Meet the commander and crew of the Valiant.
The elite intelligence force known as . . .

SPACE HAWKS

COMMANDER BRYAN KELLY. The Admiral's son whose early mission ended in disaster. *Valiant* is his chance to redeem himself . . .

DR. ANTOINETTE BEAULIEU. The brilliant but disillusioned ship's medic, she's already been forced out of the service once. She has a lot to prove . . .

CAESAR SAMMS. The only surviving member of Kelly's first command, he's tough, loyal, and battle-hardened—but his carefree lack of caution can ruin them all . . .

PHILA MOHATSA. The volatile junior operative whose secret past on a frontier planet has trained her in the use of exotic—and illegal—killing tools . . .

OLAF SIGGERSON. An older, more experienced civilian pilot, pressed into service, who rarely agrees with Commander Kelly's judgment . . .

LOUIS BAKER. An operative in disgrace sprung from the brig for the mission to Chealda. But can he be trusted?

FULL SPEED AHEAD—
ADVENTURE AWAITS!

SPACE HAWKS

Sean Dalton

ACE BOOKS, NEW YORK

This book is an Ace original edition,
and has never been previously published.

SPACE HAWKS

An Ace Book / published by arrangement with
the author

PRINTING HISTORY
Ace edition / May 1990

Cover art by Wayne Barlowe.

For information address: The Berkley Publishing Group,
200 Madison Avenue, New York, NY 10016.

ISBN: 0-441-77732-5

Ace Books are published by The Berkley Publishing Group,
200 Madison Avenue, New York, New York 10016.

PRINTED IN THE UNITED STATES OF AMERICA

10 9 8 7 6 5 4 3 2 1

1

Cmdr. Bryan Kelly inserted his AIA identity badge into the door slot and waited impatiently for the lock code to cycle through. With a click, the door opened and he limped hurriedly into the box-sized quarters that were his for the duration of his leave on Station 4. Tugging at the fastenings of his casual off-duty coveralls, he programmed a three-minute hard shower and dry. Five minutes later, swearing at the time, he emerged freshly shaven and clean with his sore muscles pounded into something resembling recovery.

Gerda, the therapy drone in the rehab center, was getting rougher every day. If he could just get past that eagle-eyed but pretty med-tech for a couple of seconds, he meant to program Gerda to ease up a bit.

Stretching to the full extent of his six-foot height, Kelly winced and shook out his dress uniform. If he didn't hurry he was going to be late for Tso's dinner party up in the officers' club. Years ago, when Kelly was fresh out of the Academy and on his first fleet assignment, he'd served with Ens. Tso Marks aboard the ESS *Wellington*. Tso was now first officer of the *Wellington*, and Kelly . . .

He smiled ruefully at his reflection in the mirror and shook his head. Shoving his hand quickly through his black hair to comb it, he straightened the set of his dress tunic across his broad shoulders. For once it was easy to fasten the stiff collar with its silver braid. Kelly frowned. He'd forgotten how much weight he'd lost.

But his tunic was cut well enough to hide that. He swept his hand across his torso, smoothing the cloth. Black and silver, with an emblem of outstretched talons on the left shoulder, the dress uniform of Special Operations was bold and distinctive. He fastened on the best of his medals: the Minzanese Silver Cross, Antares Medal of Honor, and Lexington Star Cluster.

Stepping back to study his reflection, he felt a touch of embarrassment at how resplendent he looked. As the middle son in a far from ordinary family, he'd learned early to downplay the superb Kelly abilities. To his talented family, boasting was in poor taste.

But Tso—eager to share old times—was throwing this party in honor of his wife's birthday. The price of Della's fare out here to Station 4 to share her husband's leave must have cost him a year's salary. Such an occasion called for the full effect. Kelly just hoped he could get to the officers' club without running into a lot of people.

As he headed out the door, an incoming message chime stopped him. He glanced back at the winking light and hesitated, tempted to ignore it. The chime came again.

It was probably Tso calling to tell him hurry up. Swearing, Kelly stepped back inside to the comm and snapped it on. "Kelly here."

"Compliments of Commodore West," came a live Minzanese voice over the line. "Please report to Commodore's office immediately."

Kelly frowned. For an instant the old eagerness stirred inside him, but he shook it down. They weren't due to ship out on a new mission for another two weeks. It was probably one of his squad infringing a station rule.

"Acknowledged," he said rather curtly. "Will comply."

As soon as the line cleared, he called the officers' club. "This is Commander Kelly," he said. "Please inform Lieutenant Commander Marks that I have been unavoidably delayed but will join him as soon as I can."

Hurrying out, he glimpsed his reflection as he passed and threw it a horrible grimace. What West would think of him turning up in this monkey suit didn't bear thinking about.

Halsey West's office on the uppermost level of Station 4 had the plush opulence of most deskbound brass. But West was no mere bureaucrat stuffed into a uniform. He'd served ably in the fleet for twenty years before losing a leg and arm in a Jostic ambush that shot his ship to pieces and took the lives of two-thirds of his crew. Fitted with superb bionic prosthesis limbs, the commodore nodded politely to Kelly as he came inside, slightly breathless and trying his best to cover his limp.

West was pure earthstock with his gray hair clipped so closely pink scalp gleamed through. He took in Kelly's appearance with no more than a blink.

"We appear to have interrupted your social duties, Mr. Kelly," he said in the dry, caustic tones that had cut many an erring crewman down to size. "May I introduce Fydor Ornov of the Satter Mining Consortium? Station Manager Lu'hoshoi."

Ornov and Lu'hoshoi both rose to shake hands with Kelly. The latter, wearing a traditional haircrest and colored tassles in front of his ears, clasped Kelly's fingers in the Minzanese way and bowed.

"Commander wears our warrior cross. Impressive," he said. He glanced at Ornov. "No question problem can be solved quickly."

"I'm glad you're convinced," said Ornov irritably. "I just want some action taken, gentlemen."

"Yes. Please sit down, Commander," said West. "How's the leg?"

"Rehabbing quickly, sir," said Kelly through Ornov's snort of impatience. "What seems to be the problem?"

Ornov leaned forward. "Chealda! No communications with them in the last four weeks."

Kelly dropped the last inch into his chair and sat there feeling as though he'd been socked in the solar plexus. Chealda in trouble . . . but it was an outer planet in an unimportant sector, with a climate unfriendly enough to keep most visitors away. *Dear little bro,* the message had cheerfully said six months ago. *Don't tell the family but I'm quitting my job at the lab and going out to a rotten little mining world called Chealda to do research on stress fractures. It'll keep my mind off the divorce and you know who. . . .*

"Chealda is a source of pyrillium," explained West calmly. "Located in Quadrant 3, out past—"

"*The* source," broke in Ornov curtly. "The only source

worth exploiting right now. I need not remind you, Commodore, how valuable that metal is.''

''No, you needn't,'' said West. His gaze swung to Kelly, who still hadn't gotten his breath back. ''There could be several explanations for communications silence. Power failures, ion disturbances that scramble signals—''

''Invasion, piracy, and theft!'' snapped Ornov, jumping to his feet. ''We must assume the worst. Our freighters will be launched as per schedule within three weeks to pick up this quarter's shipment stockpiled there. Chealda is ripe for robbery this time of year.''

''Excuse me, Mr. Ornov,'' said Kelly, frowning. ''But if it's been a month, why—''

''Red tape.'' Ornov scowled, turning crimson. ''Naturally we dispatched our own investigators, but they were turned back—''

''Tried to go through restricted territory,'' said West.

Kelly met his eyes and nodded. Nielson's Void lay across the shortest route between Quadrants 0 and 3. The fleet did secret weapons testing in that uninhabited section of space. It was strictly no access, even during times of emergency. *Kevalyn,* he thought, trying to hold down his alarm, *what have you gotten yourself into?*

''It's that stupid fleet mentality which has cost us time,'' Ornov was saying as he paced about West's office. ''Do you know how many litigations we've gone through to get our men and ships back from military impoundment? It's ridiculous! You people are supposed to protect us, not treat us like the enemy. And all the while Chealda is being bled dry.''

''By whom?'' ventured Lu'hoshoi unwisely.

Ornov turned on him. ''Who the hell do you think? Salukans, private raiders, who the hell cares?''

''Please, Mr. Ornov,'' said West, lifting his hand. ''No one denies that the matter must be investigated—''

''Damned right it'll be investigated,'' said Ornov. ''I've gone through every channel from the fleet admiral on down. The military is our biggest purchaser of pyrillium. You can't build good ships' hulls without it. If those mines have been compromised—''

Kelly sat forward on the edge of his chair and met the

commodore's gaze. "You want us to go, sir?" he asked quietly.

West nodded. "I'm afraid you must. It's a job for the *Wellington* if there's real trouble—"

"There is," said Ornov. "You can be sure of that."

"—but she's been stripped down for a complete refit. Manager Lu'hoshoi has spoken with the hangar chief, who says it will be eleven days until she's ready."

"And the closest active cruiser?" asked Kelly, hiding his clenched fists at his sides.

"MSS *Omu Donde*. She's on fleet maneuvers. Even at maximum speed, it will take her six days to arrive here."

"Then we'll have to go, sir," said Kelly, rising to his feet. He glanced at the station manager. "What about the *Valiant*? She can be readied fairly quickly."

Lu'hoshoi frowned in puzzlement. "*Valiant?* Not recognize name of—"

"MSS *Omu Squosa*," said West impatiently. "She's being renamed for service with Special Operations."

"Space Hawks," said Ornov, glaring at Kelly. "You boys have quite a reputation. You'd better live up to it. A lot depends on—"

"Excuse me, sir," said Kelly, glaring back. "I'm well aware of what depends—"

"Kelly," said West, and with a sharp breath Kelly pulled himself back under control.

West rose to his feet and ushered Ornov and Lu'hoshoi out, muttering assurances. Kelly remained on his feet trying not to fidget. He'd ship out tonight if he could.

"Sir," he said as soon as West returned to his desk. "With an A priority, we can get our supplies requisitioned from Stores and loaded. I'll discharge myself from rehab—"

"I've already spoken to the medic in charge of your case," said West dryly, staring deep into Kelly's eyes. "He says you're not ready."

Kelly frowned. "He's wrong. The leg's still sore, but—"

"Mentally, Kelly," broke in West. "Emotionally. You lost a ship six weeks ago. You lost three operatives. I've been there myself, boy. I know what that kind of setback takes out of a man."

Kelly glanced away, unwilling to have layers of himself

peeled back for West's scrutiny. And he sure wasn't going to tell West that Kevalyn was on Chealda. That would park him on this station for the duration of the problem.

He searched a moment for the right thing to say. Finally he met West's gaze. "Work helps, sir."

West lifted his brows. "Perhaps, but what about your squad? Two of the transferees you requested haven't arrived yet. You can't go out without a pilot. This new ship's hot with advancements in automateds, but even so I—"

"Surely there are some pilots hanging about the station," said Kelly, thinking quickly. "I could go through their qualifications. If one checks out, then—"

"Civilian pilots?" said West in astonishment. "Kelly, you're mad. I can't classify a civilian for Intelligence operations."

"You can if that pilot is sworn into the Space Hawks," said Kelly. "There's a man here, Siggerson's his name. I hear he's got quite a touch—"

"You won't get a civie to join up," said West, shaking his head. But he was already reaching for his comm. "Husho, ask Station Manager Lu'hoshoi to page all licensed pilots on the station. That's right. Priority."

West glanced at Kelly. "You still lack an operative and a medic. Ramsey's retiring. You won't get him back out on another mission. Not after that last one. He hasn't been sober in a month."

"May I see the roster, sir?"

West stared at him a moment, then put a disk in his viewer and scrolled up a list of names. "Didn't realize you were so eager to get back in harness, Kelly."

Kelly flushed and hid it by swiveling the viewer around where he could look at the roster. "I told you, sir. Work helps."

West grunted and Kelly hastily scanned through the names. "Here's a medic, sir. Antoinette Beaulieu. Assigned to Harrier Division, squad delta. She's here awaiting their next check-in. How long to process a transfer?"

West reached for his comm. "Husho, I need a transfer request filled out on one Dr. A. Beaulieu. Yes. Put her in squad alpha, Peregrine Division." He glanced at Kelly.

"That's one. Marco will have your butt when he comes in and finds his medic taken."

Kelly grinned. "He'll have to catch me first."

"There aren't any spare operatives," said West. "I've already checked. And somehow I doubt the captain of the *Wellington* will stand by while you pressgang his crew."

"What about this one? Louis Baker?''' asked Kelly. "There's a notation by his name."

West glanced at the viewer and frowned. "In the brig. He's no good. Already stripped of rank and privilege."

"What are the charges?" asked Kelly.

"Grand theft." West shook his head. "No, Kelly. I won't release him. He's a disgrace to the service and a security risk besides. He's awaiting court-martial."

"Then I have to go shorthanded."

"Against regs."

Kelly snapped off the viewer angrily. "Excuse me, sir. But do you want Chealda checked out or not? Our duty is to colonists first, not—"

"That's enough, Commander! Don't spout duty at me!" snapped West. "What good will an injured, shorthanded Space Hawk do those miners? You could go into real trouble, Kelly, and saddle us with your rescue besides—"

"No, sir," said Kelly firmly. He made up his mind to go whether West gave him authority or not. He wasn't going to sit on his thumbs and wait for a battlecruiser when Kevalyn was in trouble out there. Kelly met West's gaze. "We can do the job. We have to. You know that."

"Damn it, there's no choice," said West. He nodded reluctantly. "Consider yourself under go light, Commander."

Kelly pulled himself to attention. "Thank you, sir. And Baker?"

West scowled. "Very well. But he remains a prisoner. You watch him, Commander, and you watch your back. I don't want to hear some feeble report about how he stole your ship and left the rest of you sitting on your butts on some asteroid."

"No, sir," said Kelly. "Is that all?"

West gestured, and Kelly headed for the door. Before he reached it, however, West said, "By the way, Commander."

Kelly glanced back. "Yes?"

West's eyes were like pebbles. ''I know your sister's on Chealda. Make sure you keep your head with your assignment.''

Kelly found an unexpected lump in his throat. Swallowing it, he said gruffly, ''Thank you, sir. Would you . . . would you please send a code nine message to my father? He's on maneuvers with the 5th Earth Fleet.''

West lifted his thumb in the centuries' old gesture of good luck, and Kelly hurried out.

2

A maintenance crew of mostly Minzanese all talking at once crowded the quarterdeck of the *Valiant*, pulling down panels, chattering into communicators, and heaping a myriad of complicated instructions onto Siggerson as the minutes counted down to cast off.

The quarterdeck itself, gleaming with pristine newness, formed a U with six station seats arranged around a large, rectangular astrogation board currently lit a soft green but not yet showing any star maps. The power boards were lighting up in steady progression as the automated systems came on-line. Gravity and life support had already been switched off the battery reserves although the engines were barely warming.

Tremendous, effortless power, Kelly thought. He'd already listened to Siggerson rhapsodizing over her power utilization curves, and the gist of it all was that he had the fastest ship in the fleet. Power, speed, toughness . . . that's what he asked from a ship, but in spite of himself he could feel that this vessel was special.

Cut the fantasies, he told himself. *She's just new. She smells good. Wait until the air recycles a couple of times and she gets that same old stench they all have.*

He yawned and rubbed his face. His eyes felt gritty from a lack of sleep and his leg ached all the way down. He thought about the packet of little green tablets in his cabin and shoved the temptation away. Painkillers could become a crutch. He'd rest once they were underway.

"I keep getting an odd ghost reading on these internal sensor checks," Siggerson was saying.

Kelly forced himself to listen. "They're still loading equipment. Why don't you hold that test until we cast off?"

Siggerson sighed. He was thin and going bald, with pale freckled skin and reddish brown hair. His eyes were expressionless, like pebbles. So far he appeared to be a man who spoke only when necessary, got hung up on details, and demanded perfection.

"I don't like glitches," he said. "Especially this early. It should be traced down—"

"We don't have time," said Kelly.

Siggerson looked at him as though he were a fool. "And what happens twenty parsecs out, when this glitch stops masking a real problem and we find ourselves—"

"Permission to come onto the quarterdeck," said a woman's contralto.

Turning, Kelly saw a rangy black woman with short, graying hair and imperious eyes standing upon the ladder. *Too old,* thought Kelly in dismay.

"Permission granted," he said hollowly.

She emerged from the turnaround and came across the quarterdeck toward him. Her black duty coveralls with the bold silver stripe across the torso were stiff and new. She didn't bother to give her state-of-the-art surroundings more than a cursory glance. As she halted before Kelly, he saw the medical staff clutched in the talons of her Hawk emblem. He frowned, still hoping she might be anyone but Beaulieu.

Her own eyes flashed with anger. "Commander Kelly, I presume?"

He nodded.

"Dr. Beaulieu reporting." Her voice was brusque. "I want to protest this arbitrary transfer. I was assigned to the Harrier Division."

Irritation surfaced in Kelly. Old *and* a complainer. "That's the luck of the draw, Doctor," he said. "In the service you go where you're sent."

She snorted. "I served on the fleet active list for over twenty years, Commander. I know how the process works. I also know personnel stealing when I see it."

Kelly's brows rose. "Harrier squad delta isn't coming in for another fifteen days. I need a medic now."

"Obviously," she said, glancing at the hurried activity surrounding them. "The fact remains that I'm not ready. I still have five orientation sessions to complete and training on—"

"You look fit enough," he said, trying not to lose patience. "Special Operations isn't that much different from fleet service."

"That's a simplistic view," she retorted. "I do a good job, Commander, but only when I'm properly prepared. I don't—"

"Look, Doctor," he broke in, shifting his weight to reach for the cargo report Caesar was trying to hand him past a knot of arguing technicians.

Kelly ran his eye swiftly down the items and noticed they were short on equipment. He frowned and glanced at Caesar, who opened his mouth. Kelly shook his head sharply and returned his attention to Beaulieu.

"Preparation is less important to me right now than your presence. We are responding to a potential emergency in which lives may be at stake. Now, frankly, I don't care whether you've completed any of those blasted orientation sessions as long as you know your job and can do it."

Her head came up, and some of the fire banked down in her eyes. "I see," she said in a slightly different tone. "No one took the trouble to explain the situation to me. Of course I will do my job. I—"

"Good," he said, moving away from her. "Sickbay is located on the lower deck. Please check it out immediately to verify that you have all the supplies you need. We cast off in thirty-six minutes."

She looked disconcerted by his abrupt dismissal, but he was already turning to Caesar, who had been an operative in his squad from the very first day and ought to know better than to bring him a cargo sheet like this.

"Now, Boss," said Caesar, lifting his hands in mock innocence. "Don't pin me to the wall with those baby blues. We've got some peculiar space limitations in the hold, which isn't a hold at all but a closet squeezed in beside some enormous power batteries."

Siggerson turned away from the sensor panel he was testing. "Reserves," he said. "XKy models. Real beauties with almost no natural drain. They're precisely compatible with this photonic drive—''

''Do you mind?'' said Caesar, and Siggerson returned to his work with a shrug. ''Like I'm saying, Boss, a closet. It's going to take time to measure our usual stockpile and figure out how to maximize our space. I've been estimating because of our deadline, see, and—''

''Hand scanners,'' said Kelly, refusing to be pacified, ''do not take up much space.''

Caesar grimaced and scratched his head where red hair grew in an unruly thatch. ''Nooo,'' he said, drawing it out. ''But the station quartermaster says they're out.''

''What?''

''The shipment hasn't arrived yet.''

''Couldn't you turn some up?''

''If I had more time I could make a deal with the quartermaster on the *Wellington*,'' said Caesar. ''But—'' He shrugged.

''What about the arsenal?'' said Kelly, scrolling the list. ''A bit heavy on explosives. Especially this gel. Where we're going, it'll be too cold for that to set up properly.''

''But it's good stuff,'' said Caesar in concern. ''New and twice as—''

''More charge clips and Klopers,'' said Kelly firmly, handing back the list. ''You can use the gel another time. Did you get a short cannon?''

Caesar nodded, still looking unhappy as he crossed off the gel. ''It's coming. I got it off—''

''Never mind,'' said Kelly hastily as Siggerson shot them a glance and a couple of technicians stopped talking. Short cannons were illegal munitions commonly used by private traders who felt the fines were a small price to pay for the protection they offered. ''Where's Baker?''

''Still shifting things around.'' Caesar's green eyes grew troubled. ''Say, Boss, about this guy . . .''

''I know,'' said Kelly. ''Keep the arsenal locked and don't issue him a prong.''

''He's under criminal charges, isn't he?'' Caesar shook his head. ''Since when do we go out with brig bilge?''

Kelly frowned, aware that Baker could cause trouble with the rest of the squad. ''This time, Caesar. That's all.''

But Caesar stood his ground. "And what about him?" he asked softly, jerking a thumb at Siggerson's back. "A civie pilot. Yusus, Boss! And that baby, Mohatsa. She's easy on the eyes, but she doesn't know a thing. Orders or not, we're just not ready. We can't depend on any of these squats. And you're—"

"I'm fine," said Kelly shortly.

"You look worn out."

Kelly drew in a quick breath, then hauled his temper under control. Caesar had been with him long enough to take liberties like this. Caesar was also right. Still, there wasn't anything he could do.

"See to those changes, Operative Samms," he said.

Caesar shrugged, giving up. "Right, Boss. But I just got a bad feeling about this."

Kelly did too, but he knew better than to encourage Caesar. He forced himself to smile. "File it under Celtic moodiness and get back to work."

"Soyo."

"Oh, and, Caesar?"

Samms glanced back.

"Watch your back with Baker."

Caesar nodded. "He ought to be jettisoned with our first garbage emission."

"Kelly," said Siggerson. "Time to clear ship."

Kelly nodded and started to tell him to carry on, then hesitated. Olaf Siggerson's light brown eyes stared at him with a lack of anything but impatience. He wasn't sworn in, he didn't have to call anyone sir, and technically he couldn't give orders.

"This is too awkward," said Kelly. "For the duration of this mission I'm granting you temporary rank of lieutenant commander."

Siggerson just went on looking at him without much expression. "Have you the authority to do so?"

"As soon as the hatch seals, I do," said Kelly. "As of now I consider the hatch sealed. Carry on, Mr. Siggerson."

Siggerson didn't show if he was pleased or not. He simply opened a comm line through the ship. "Clear the ship, please. All technicians clear the ship. Hatches will seal in five minutes from this mark."

The people mobbing the quarterdeck shut panels and gathered their clutter of tools and scanners. It took time for them to file down the ladder one by one.

Siggerson tossed aside the abbreviated operations manual he'd been clutching since he came aboard and dropped into his station seat. Slumping there, with his thin body looking like a pile of bones thrown together, he began humming softly to himself as his hands flew over the sensor controls.

Kelly watched him in surprise. "Another test?"

"Last check."

"For what?" asked Kelly. "You're going to wear out the systems before we get started."

Siggerson grunted without looking up. "Doesn't show now. Internal scans check clean."

"Good," said Kelly, glad they'd seen the last of Siggerson's glitch. He took the intership comm. "All hands, report to quarterdeck."

They came up the ladder by the time Siggerson had the external hatches sealing. The airlock jettisoned its atmosphere, and the interior of the ship repressurized, causing gentle poppings inside Kelly's ears.

Baker and Mohatsa took their seats, and a panting Caesar handed Kelly an amended cargo sheet.

"Best I could do, Boss," he said, wiping his face.

Beaulieu, still looking too crisp and new, stood behind him with her own check sheet. "An excellent sickbay facility, Commander, for its size."

Kelly, impatient to be gone, tossed the sheets aside. "Commence final run-through to castoff, Mr. Siggerson."

Right on schedule, the wedge-shaped *Valiant* turned on her running lights and sounded the warning. Kelly sat on the edge of his seat, refusing to strap in, and watched their departure on the viewscreen. Behind him, he could hear the chatter of hangar control over the open comm. Unlike a battlecruiser, where the helmsman was actually responsible for powering his vessel from her berth, the *Valiant* was small enough to be tractored out.

"Moorings off," said Siggerson. "Relinquishing to external control."

All they had to do at that point was sit back and watch. A badly battered destroyer flashed her running lights in salute as they passed her, and Kelly found an inexplicable lump in his throat. He glanced around at the faces of his squad as they watched the screen, enrapt. For the first time it really came home to him that Arness, Rugie, and Stokes were gone. How many missions had they tackled together? How many jokes had they shared? How many disappointments? How many leaves? Their ghosts swarmed him.

"Boss? Hey, Boss!" called Caesar.

The ghosts faded, and Kelly blinked a moment, feeling breathless. His gaze fastened on Caesar's homely face.

Caesar smiled, showing the missing teeth he'd lost in innumerable bar brawls and never troubled to replace. He lifted his thumb.

"Swift flight and home again," he said solemnly. It was the ritual blessing of the Hawks.

Awkwardly they all repeated it, Mohatsa stumbling through the words with a flush, Beaulieu's husky voice covering hers, Baker showing cynical boredom as his gaze roved in open assessment of the others, Siggerson with absolute indifference.

Ahead, the hangar doors were sliding open just enough to allow the *Valiant* to exit. Kelly felt a slight lurch in the ship as the tractor released them. Most pilots let inertia carry them through the doors. A few preferred to show off their skills by kicking in sublight power and shooting out with a colorful ion trail. The *Valiant*, however, had no fuel emissions to leave behind. Kelly wondered what Siggerson would do, and seconds later Siggerson answered that by engaging power smoothly and skimming out in a graceful arc that wasted not a single degree of trajectory.

"Thank you, Mr. Siggerson," said Kelly in admiration. "Set shortest course for Chealda."

The astrogation board flashed up a star map with an indicator already blinking in red.

"Coordinates locked in. Automateds switching over." Siggerson glanced up calmly. "Strap in, please."

"This isn't a passenger liner, Siggie," said Caesar in protest.

Siggerson ignored him. "Switching to interstellar shields. Prepare for distort."

Most of Kelly's doubts about Siggerson were fading fast.

That dry, laconic voice was both confident and reassuring. Kelly, like most veteran Hawks, preferred to go into distort without strapping down. But he couldn't give Siggerson permission to issue orders, then not support him. Kelly reached for his harness and glared at Caesar until he did the same.

Kelly glanced at his other people and noticed that Beaulieu had managed to decipher the controls to her medical readouts and sat ready to watch the monitors. Phila Mohatsa, a small woman with a long curly mane of black hair and almond-shaped eyes, watched the viewscreen intently. Baker looked half asleep but his eyes never left Mohatsa. Feeling a surge of protectiveness, Kelly frowned.

He glanced at Siggerson. "Let's go."

Siggerson had his gaze on the astrogation board where it belonged. A pilot couldn't afford to watch the rainbow effect of time distortion that sparkled upon the viewscreen as they engaged full power and leapt across the curve of space.

An audible sigh escaped Mohatsa as they watched the stars and constellations shift and huddle in the aberration effect, blurring before them. Blues and violet melted before them, spreading the light spectrum. Then Siggerson switched the viewscreen to override the distortion and showed them a simulacrum of how the constellations should look. Mohatsa sighed again and glanced around.

"I love it," she said. "I never get tired of seeing it. Like poetry, don't you think?"

Then she caught Kelly's gaze upon her. She reddened a bit, but her dark eyes remained unashamed. He smiled, and she relaxed visibly.

She was off a colony planet, probably an agriculture one although he hadn't read her record closely yet. Academy trained, but no officer's school. She'd gone straight over to the Hawks upon finishing, and here she was, looking impossibly young and eager and green. Except that she carried her prong up her sleeve for quick access. Maybe she wasn't as green as he thought.

Abruptly Kelly jerked the release of his harness. "All hands, free time. Mr. Siggerson, set up your relief schedule and we'll adhere to the assignments. I'll post an activity chart later."

"Turning in, boss?" asked Caesar, standing up to stretch.

Kelly didn't miss the concern under his casual tone. Caesar's fussing was uncharacteristic, and it irritated Kelly. But he hid it as he said, "That's right. It's been a long twenty-six hours."

"It may be longer," said Siggerson grimly. "I'm picking up that ghost reading across my data again."

"All right, Baker," said Caesar angrily, turning on him. "Who have you stowed aboard?"

"Nobody, squat," said Baker, raking Caesar with an insolent look. He moved toward the turnaround, but paused beside Kelly. "When do I get my weapons issue?"

Kelly looked into colorless eyes that seemed to have no depth at all. They were chilling, conscienceless. He kept his own expression neutral as he replied, "You don't. Not until we go into action."

Baker protested angrily. "That's not fair! I'm on active duty, same as everyone else. I'm still a Hawk. I—"

"You," said Kelly coldly, "are a disgrace to the uniform you wear. You are not the same as everyone else. No weapons."

"That's—"

"Be glad you've got your liberty," said Kelly, and Baker quieted at the implied threat.

With a mutter, Baker climbed down the ladder. There was a moment of tense silence afterward. Mohatsa and Beaulieu both looked startled. Kelly hesitated, then made his decision. He hadn't kept things from his former squad; there was no point in changing that habit now, especially if he wanted to mold these individuals into a team.

"It's no secret," he said. "Baker faces stiff charges back on Station 4. He shouldn't be in uniform and he shouldn't be on duty with us, except that there wasn't another operative. All of you, watch yourselves. Keep your cabins locked if you wish. I realize there's no way a squad can function well without mutual trust, but he won't be with us after this mission. I apologize for this state of affairs, but the emergency on Chealda has priority over temporary discomfort. Just be careful. If you need anything from the arsenal or stores, let Caesar know and he'll give you access. That's all."

"What about our stowaway?" said Siggerson.

Kelly sighed. He was too tired to care right now. "Mohatsa, you and Samms do a search. We might as well clear this up."

Leaving them, he made his way to his cabin where his duffle rested on his bunk. The space was lean and designed for maximum efficiency. Muted gold and buff provided soothing colors. A Minzanese airlace stood in the corner, its delicate, dark green fronds unfolding as Kelly moved about stowing his few personal items. He hadn't much. His collection of Salukan swords and daggers had been destroyed with the old ship, along with the Boxcan primitive rain masks and a priceless small sculpture of bard crystal. Somehow he hadn't felt like shopping for replacements on Station 4.

Finishing, he glanced around. He had a bunk, a desk with a viewer, and a minuscule head. The cabin looked austere. It did not feel like home. Wondering if it ever would, he stretched out on his bunk and stared at the ceiling as the lights dimmed. His body craved sleep, but his mind refused to rest.

Three days at maximum speed to Chealda. That's if the *Valiant* could really hold a constant cruising speed of TD 10. In the meantime, speculating as to what was wrong there would only waste time and drive him nuts. Kevalyn could hold out for three more days. He had to believe that.

3

"Commander," said Phila Mohatsa, "we're picking up an outside transmission."

On one side of the quarterdeck, Caesar and Baker paused in their poker game. Kelly looked up from reading an account of Hannibal's greatest battle and frowned in sudden alertness.

"Traffic chatter?"

"No, sir," she said. "I was just scanning the signal waves for fun. This is catching on the outermost sweep—"

"Bring it in."

She nodded and more of the communications board came to life. "Too faint. I can't grab it. Siggerson, boost more, how about?"

Siggerson, who'd progressed from the abbreviated ship's manual to the complete one, flipped a switch without looking up from his reading.

"Got it," said Phila. "Switching to speakers."

A burst of static filled the air. But underneath it ran the unmistakable signal of a standard distress call.

"Siggerson," said Kelly. "Pick that vessel up on the sensors. What is it and where?"

Siggerson got to work. After a few minutes, he glanced over his shoulder. "Beyond firm sensor range. Here's where it is."

Blue indicators winked on the astrogation table. They gathered around, and Caesar loosed a low whistle.

"Way off our course, Boss."

Kelly stared at the gap between their own heading and the ship in distress. He wanted to swear, to ignore it, to ask Phila to seek another ship in the area that could answer that call for them, but they were alone out here.

"Adjust course, Mr. Siggerson," he said, his fists closing at his sides. "We will respond."

Siggerson nodded and went to work.

"Commander," said Phila challengingly. "Do we forget Chealda? Caesar says your sister is there."

Kelly flushed. He hadn't had to prove himself to a squad in a long time. They were watching him now, measuring him. He knew they wondered if he was a man to follow.

Glaring at Caesar, he said, "Chealda is a matter of investigation, not a declared emergency. We can't let it take priority over a distress call." His eyes shifted back to Phila. "You should know that."

Her gaze dropped. "Yes, sir."

Kelly went back to glaring at Caesar. "As for gossiping, Operative Samms—"

Caesar lifted his hands. "Now, Boss. I figured everyone should know. Your rule has always been not to shoulder things alone while on a mission. I didn't know that had changed."

Kelly winced, and his anger faded. He glanced at their watchful faces. Caesar was right. An operative brooding about personal problems was an operative with half his mind on his job. And that could get people killed. Kelly knew he had no excuse to be breaking that rule himself. But they were strangers—mismatched and lacking camaraderie.

And how will they ever team up and trust each other, he thought, *if you don't start the example?*

"All right," he said gruffly. "The rule Caesar's talking about is one I've always had for my squads. My trouble is that I had a crack team for three years and some of them were killed two months ago. We knew and trusted each other. We'd worked together so long we could tell exactly how each of us thought. You don't get that kind of trust overnight. But I'd like for this squad to become just as good or better."

"Then you could start by trusting me," said Baker. "And giving me weapons like everyone else."

"Shut up, brig bilge," said Caesar.

"Yeah?" retorted Baker. "Just because I've played the black market a little doesn't make me something you can step on every chance you get, Samms. I'm as good an operative as you—any of you!'' His eyes swept them. ''I had a record when I joined the Space Hawks. They said they'd overlook my past if I'd do my job.''

''Don't make us cry,'' said Caesar. ''You weren't supposed to go on stealing.''

Baker shrugged. ''So what? All I know is, the Hawks are supposed to be a good deal, where everyone gets treated the same. That's *scatsi*, that is. Here we are with an admiral's son, running off to some dustball on the backside of nowhere to rescue his sister. What about—''

''We aren't going to Chealda because of Kevalyn,'' said Kelly. ''She happens to be there along with eight hundred other people. And it's her tough luck.''

Phila laughed a little harshly. ''You don't really expect us to believe that.''

''Kelly's fair,'' said Caesar hotly. ''You get that straight now.''

Phila shot Kelly a look of calculation. ''We could pretend we didn't pick up this distress call. Maybe my ears play tricks on me sometimes.''

Baker looked shocked. ''You can't ignore a distress call. That's—''

Caesar gripped Baker's arm to shut him up. His green eyes smiled into Kelly's. ''Sure, Boss,'' he said. ''Who's going to know?''

''We will,'' said Kelly. He forced out a breath, pushing temptation with it, and glared at Phila. ''You've tested me enough, Operative Mohatsa. There won't be any more of these games.''

Her cheeks reddened. ''No, sir.''

''New course laid in,'' said Siggerson. ''Do I take it or not?''

Kelly glanced at him. ''Yes. Execute.''

She was a battered old ore freighter that looked too decrepit to be functional. Black scoring marked her sides, and the rear center section of her hull showed a jagged split. She made crooked progress, showing no evidence of holding a course.

Gathered at the viewscreen of the *Valiant*, they watched her.

"A wanderer," said Caesar in disgust. "Probably the only thing working on her is that beacon. We really should have ignored her."

"We never have that option in space, Mr. Samms," said Kelly sharply. But his throat was locked up tight with frustration. All this way off their course for nothing.

Baker shook his head. "We could tow her in for the salvage price. Maybe she still has cargo." He hesitated and glanced at Kelly. "After Chealda, I mean."

"I'm getting life readings," said Siggerson.

Kelly blinked. "How many?" he asked.

"Twenty . . . no . . ." Siggerson scowled and cleared his data input with an angry swipe of his hand. "Damn that ghost! It's crossing my data again. If you'd done a proper search of the ship, Samms—"

"I did," said Caesar hotly. "Nothing. You just can't chase down your glitch, Siggie. Don't blame it on me."

"Belay that, both of you," snapped Kelly. "If there are people on that vessel, they need help. How's life support over there?"

Siggerson scowled at his instrumentation. "Barely functional. There's atmosphere. Some heat. All the readings are at the same location. They've probably gathered in one place to conserve energy."

Mohatsa looked up. "They don't respond to hailing frequencies."

"Ah!" said Caesar, bouncing on his toes. "Hostiles. Maybe we've found a nest of Jostics."

Baker backed up. "Then let's get 'em! Teleport a couple of bombs over and—"

"Samms and Mohatsa will investigate," said Kelly. He glanced at each of them in turn. "Kit up and report to the teleport bay. Siggerson, move us closer. I want to parallel that freighter."

"We can't dock-link with her," said Siggerson sharply.

"I haven't suggested that we do so. Carry out my instructions, Mr. Siggerson."

Siggerson looked disconcerted. "Very well."

Caesar and Phila crossed the quarterdeck to the turnaround and started down the ladder. Kelly followed, stopping off on his way to the teleport bay to talk to Beaulieu.

The sickbay was slightly larger than his own cabin. It contained two beds and a life support capsule in addition to a highly sophisticated biology computer and a re-gen system for quick patching up of broken bones and lacerations. The colors of the walls and floor were soft shades of foam green, like the oceans on Minza. The color of life. Beaulieu was working her way through dense-looking text on her viewer. She turned as he came in and rose to her feet.

"We've arrived," said Kelly. "It's a damaged ore freighter, carrying perhaps twenty people."

She nodded. "I'll get my medikit."

"Not yet." Kelly raised his hand. "I'm sending Samms and Mohatsa over to check things out. As soon as they've established the situation, you'll go. I wanted to give you as much warning as possible."

"Thank you, but I practice instant readiness." Her head lifted proudly. "You don't have to coddle me."

She read him too easily. Kelly flushed. "Medics aren't used as cannon fodder. You know that, Doctor."

It was her turn to look embarrassed. Awkward silence fell between them.

"Look," said Kelly at last, deciding it was up to him to smooth out this problem. "I've had time to go through your record. I know the fleet kicked you out into retirement. You couldn't stand the softness of civilian life, and you came back in with us. I admit I thought you were too old for the job when I first saw you, but that's an unfair judgment to make this early in the game."

Her cheeks darkened. "I wasn't aware there was a probation period in Special Operations. I passed the physical and mental exams. I passed security checks. I even had to retake my medical boards. I could be teaching at the University of Human Sciences instead of running around out here risking my neck. How long do I have to keep proving myself?"

"You don't," Kelly said quietly. "It's hard for me to get used to the idea that your predecessor's not around. That has nothing to do with you, and it's my problem."

She met his gaze, and the fierceness in her eyes faded slightly. "Well, well," she said softly. "So you are human, after all. I was beginning to wonder."

"I might say the same about you."

They glared at each other, then Kelly frowned. "We're being childish. Can we start over?"

"People don't start over, Commander," she said briskly. "They just change directions. Perhaps I should tell you I have separate orders from West to keep an eye on you."

Kelly blinked angrily. If that was her idea of a truce overture, he'd just as soon forget the whole thing.

"West is worrying for nothing," he said. "I'm not going to crack up."

"You lost people close to you, and your sister is in danger. Those are strong pressures."

He shook his head, wishing he'd just called her to the teleport bay instead of coming here. With his operatives already second-guessing him at every step, the last thing he needed was a medic trying to take his head apart.

"Don't look so defensive," she said. "I'm not the kind of doctor who follows you around with monitors. Just don't try to stand on the ice alone. If you need help, ask me for it."

He let out his breath in surprise. "That's fair. You have a deal, Doctor."

She picked up her medikit. "I might as well wait in the teleport bay until it's safe for me to go over."

Caesar and Phila were already on the teleport platform when Kelly and Beaulieu arrived. Phila held her sidearm pointed at the ceiling in readiness. Caesar had his tucked in the crook of his arm while he struggled to fasten on his wristband communicator.

"Come on, Samms," Phila was saying impatiently. "What do you have, three thumbs?"

She broke off at the sight of Kelly. Caesar swore at his wristband and finally got it on.

"Ready, Boss," he said sheepishly. "Me and White Lightning here are a go."

Going to the control bank, Kelly pushed activation. Lights came on around Caesar's and Phila's feet. "Have you entered your wristband codes into the system?"

"Yo, Boss," said Caesar with a yawn. "Siggie's already sent the coordinates down the pike. Maybe we'll materialize in someone's shower."

Kelly grinned. "Watch yourselves," he said and touched the control.

They shimmered out. Beaulieu walked over to buckle on a wristband. Silence followed. Kelly frowned. Standard procedure called for immediate check-in. He looked over the systems to make sure the comm was working.

After five interminable minutes, Kelly grew tense with worry. This was too long a lag for check-in time.

"What are they doing over there?"

Beaulieu glanced up. "A problem?"

Kelly touched the comm. "*Valiant* to Samms. Come in!"

"Boss?" replied Caesar's voice. "In and safe."

Kelly let out his breath. "You might say so a little sooner. What's the situation?"

"Grim," said Caesar. "You and Doc better come over."

For once Caesar did not exaggerate. Kelly and Beaulieu materialized into a gloomy hellhole. The air stank of urine and desperation. The temperature was only a few degrees above freezing. Kelly shivered as he glanced around, squinting in an effort to see. A single light panel in this chamber remained functional, and it flickered a muted glow, looking as though it would fail at any minute. Bodies lay everywhere, piled on top of each other in huddles for warmth. Here and there about the room a few individuals stirred, rising from beneath tattered blankets to stare at the squad.

"They've come," said a thin, feeble voice. "They've found us."

"No, Hamar. It's your stomach sending you visions again."

Appalled at such deprivation, Kelly stepped forward.

"We're not hallucinations," he said loudly. "I am Commander Kelly of Special Operations. We have come in response to your distress call. Please identify yourselves and tell us how we may help."

More heads wavered up. A hand clutched Kelly's ankle. He crouched by the man who was trying to sit up.

"Easy," Kelly said gently. "Conserve your strength."

"We're . . . from Chealda," gasped the man. "Refugees. Satter Mining Consortium. Please . . . help us . . ."

"Chealda!" said Kelly. "We were on our way there when we picked up your signal. What's happened? You—"

"Not yet, Commander," said Beaulieu, brushing him

aside. She unclipped her medikit from her belt and activated a hand scanner. "This man is suffering from starvation and what looks like a good start on pneumonia. We need heat and light set up in here."

"But I must find out what's happened to them," said Kelly.

Her eyes flicked to his. "Not yet."

Frustrated, he backed away and called the ship. "Kelly to *Valiant*."

Siggerson's voice responded.

"We need food sent over," said Kelly. "All the supplies we can spare."

"And water," said Beaulieu, moving to another victim. "Water first."

"I heard," said Siggerson. "Anything else?"

"Yes. Send Baker over with porta-lamps. We've got to see before we can start systems repairs."

"Do you need me?"

"Probably," said Kelly wryly. Engineering was not his best area. "But I think Mohatsa can handle things. I want you to stay with the ship. Send a message to Commodore West. Tell him we've found refugees fleeing Chealda and to send out a rescue ship immediately."

"Can do."

"Keep an open link for questions. We may need a tie to the computers. And what about that repair drone in storage? Can it be activated and used over here?"

"Negative. Too specialized. Besides, I don't think you'll get her powered up again," said Siggerson. "Looks like she took a severe hit in the engine area. It would be too dangerous to try to spark the antimatter pods anyway. You'd better concentrate on recharging her reserve cells. They're nearly depleted, and if they go, she'll be dead forever."

"Stand by," said Kelly and broke contact. He glanced around at Caesar and Phila. "Let's get started."

"The engines are aft," said Caesar, jerking his thumb over his shoulder. "Sealed off by an emergency bulkhead. Beyond that, she's split wide open. I could cut us a hole, but then we'd have to set up a blister field to contain internal atmosphere, and we aren't equipped for that. Plus, we'll have to work in suits and I doubt it's worth the trouble. She's pretty shot up."

"If Siggerson will send over one of his systems scanners and a tool kit," said Phila, shaking back her hair, "I can check the integrity of the electrical system from here."

She was acting like a trained operative now instead of a punk. Kelly nodded, revising his estimate of her. "Great. Caesar, make the call."

The area they were in had apparently been the ship's lounge. Phila headed across it, and Kelly followed, taking care not to step on anyone. Someone was moaning. A child began to cry in a thin wail despite its mother's attempts to hush it. Hands reached out to him.

"Help us. Please, help us."

"Yes," said Kelly, gripping a bony shoulder. He crouched down to peer into that desperate face. "We will. You'll be all right now. Tell me, is a scientist named Kevalyn Miscetti aboard?"

But the woman began to cry instead, and he could get nothing from her. Patting her shoulder, Kelly went on to bend over a young man who had wrapped his arms about himself and was rocking in a kind of desperate frenzy.

"Who did this to you?" he asked. "What happened? Who attacked your ship?"

The man went on rocking. His eyes stared through Kelly. "We'll have to eat them soon," he whispered. "Don't tell Annya. The dead ones . . . we'll have to eat them soon."

Kelly drew away abruptly, horrified. If they had been reduced to cannibalism, better not ask too many questions about it.

A natural disaster of some kind on Chealda? Or an invasion? Ornov's fears certainly looked justified now. Would the Salukans dare invade Alliance territory, risking war, just to make a raid for pyrillium? How would they have gotten past Chealda's sophisticated defense system? It was supposed to notify Fleet Headquarters of any breach.

Kelly looked at Phila in frustration. "I've got to know what happened to them!"

"Yeah." She pulled her prong from her sleeve and snapped out one of its three blades. "But they aren't in shape to answer questions yet. Maybe having the lights on will help."

Kelly nodded, getting himself back under control. "A whole team of medics would be even better."

"Oh, Beaulieu's good, sir," said Phila, slipping the edge of her knife beneath the corner of the panel. "One of my classmates at Academy had an uncle who served with her on the *Nemesis*."

One practiced twist of her wrist and the corner popped loose. She loosened the remaining three corners in quick succession, and Kelly lifted down the panel for her. Pocketing her prong with a swift sleight of hand that Kelly admired, she peered into the recess and snorted.

"Too dark. Caesar! Where's that equipment?"

"Coming, toots," said Caesar, struggling to step over people. "Keep your pants on."

"*Viti, mandale!* I could have this fixed by now. Throw the scanner to the commander." She paused and withdrew her head from the recess to look at Kelly uncertainly. "Sorry, sir."

Kelly grinned and gave her a light slap on her shoulder. "Phila, you're the electronics expert. I'm only here to help."

She grinned back, her black eyes warming. "Hokay, sir. Catch that scanner, will you?"

Kelly turned and gestured to Caesar, who tossed the entire tool kit. Kelly caught it with a grunt and opened it to rummage for the scanner. He handed it over, and Phila's head disappeared into the recess.

"We can get light," she said, her voice muffled, "but it will take time. I'll have to trace out that circuit with a laser probe. Something really shorted out the system, but part of it's intact."

Caesar came up to Kelly. "Baker's on his way with the porta-lamps and food. It took awhile to convince him that this wasn't a Jostic trap."

"You put the idea into his head," said Kelly, trying not to fidget. He frowned at Phila's back.

Emerging again, she picked up a laser probe and jabbed something with quick delicacy. The lights overhead flickered, then went out again. A ragged cheer went around the room.

"Almost," said Phila. "If we don't care about what happens to the system, which is crisped to hell anyway, then I can . . ."

The lights came on and stayed on. Refugees sat up, blinking and shielding their eyes. Kelly glanced around at their haggard faces. He counted fifteen people and two children.

Kevalyn was not among them. Kelly rubbed his jaw, not certain whether to be more worried or relieved.

Placing the handle of the laser probe between her teeth, Phila squinted critically at her work. "This won't last long," she said. "I'll have to get to the next relay and jury-rig it."

Grabbing the tool kit off the floor, she hurried along the wall to the next panel. Kelly and Caesar exchanged glances.

"She ain't bad, Boss."

"No, she isn't," agreed Kelly. "Use your prong to help pry the rest of these panels loose. And start looking for a main power line through here."

"This tub's dead, Boss. Very dead."

"I know, but if we can get even a nudge out of her we might be able to stop her from drifting."

From the corner of his eye, he saw Baker materializing in a shimmer of blue and silver light. A stack of equipment clustered around Baker's feet.

"Well, well," said Caesar. "The Queen of Sheba arrives at last."

Kelly glanced at him. "You'd better hustle if you're going to keep up with Mohatsa."

"Yusus, Boss. You know I've got six thumbs when it comes to this kind of work. Wrecking, not repairing, is my—"

Kelly made a shooing motion, and Caesar went off. Kelly made his way over to Baker, who was staring at the sight around him with a grimace.

"God, what a stink," said Baker. "Who are these cre—"

"That'll do, Baker," said Kelly. "Get busy setting up the lamps. Then you can help Dr. Beaulieu in passing out rations. See that distribution is small but fair. Don't let them get out of hand."

"If you want me to keep them under control, then I need a sidearm the same as everyone else," said Baker.

Furious, Kelly grabbed his arm. "These are civilians, not prisoners. They need help and care and kindness. You will give it to them."

Baker's cynical eyes met his indifferently. "Whatever you say." Pulling free, he began opening canisters.

An exhausting five hours later, enough repairs had been made on the freighter to strengthen her life support systems to more bearable conditions. Food and water seemed to be taking care of the rest, although many of the refugees had injuries—mostly broken bones and burns. Beaulieu continued to move tirelessly among them, checking quietly with her scanner, offering comfort to those awake and restless.

Smeared with coolant and grime, Kelly sat down with Hamar in a corner. Wrapped in a silver-colored survival blanket, Hamar looked like a small, shrunken mummy. He nursed a mug of steaming coffee in his unsteady hands.

''Now,'' said Kelly, ''tell me as simply as you can about the situation on Chealda.''

''Salukans,'' said Hamar, blinking as though the lights still hurt his eyes. ''They came weeks ago—''

''But how? Your defense satellites—''

''Ineffective,'' said Hamar. ''As for our warning systems mounted in orbit . . .'' He shook his head and shrugged. ''Useless. We thought ourselves safe. But one morning we woke up to find an invasion force upon us. The employees of Kuupke Smelter tried to fight. They were all killed. The rest of us surrendered.'' He dropped his gaze from Kelly's. ''What could we do? We aren't fighters.''

''No,'' said Kelly, still finding it hard to believe the Salukans would dare break the treaty like this. ''Please go on.''

''Our stockpile of pyrillium is the best we've had since coming to Chealda. Gone now. The Salukans have loaded all of it. Our company freighters will have to go back empty for the first time in—''

''Are the Salukans still there?'' asked Kelly.

''Oh, yes.'' Hamar looked bitter. ''Stealing the shipments wasn't enough. Now they are forcing the miners to work past human endurance to collect as much of the raw ore as they can. They know when the company freighters are scheduled to come. By then those devils will be gone.''

Kelly was puzzled. How had Salukans gotten this deep into Alliance territory without detection?

A flush darkened Hamar's sunken cheeks. ''They are monsters, indifferent to the lives they've squandered. We're nothing to them. Insects. Even the children have been put into the mines to work.''

''How did you get away?''

"They destroyed our TemStar communications satellite when they arrived," said Hamar. "We couldn't call for help."

Kelly frowned, but let himself be diverted. "Obviously the Salukans planned to come in, take what they wanted, and leave no trace. You're in an isolated sector. Patrols don't check by often. Where is most of the population distributed?"

"We're only on the western continent," said Hamar, sipping his coffee. "The company hasn't sunk exploration shafts elsewhere yet. The glaciers are too thick. But we—"

"Are the research labs located independently of the mining operations?"

"No."

Kelly glanced away to mask his worry.

"There's only one place for research, and that's at Caru Refinery. They get an oil product often when they strike a vein of pyrillium, and many of the underdeveloped worlds still on the combustion engine level buy from us." Hamar sighed. "They took that too."

"How big is the Salukan force?"

Hamar shrugged. "I don't know. Big enough, obviously. Troopers and—"

"How many ships?"

Hamar glared at him. "How did they get to us? Where were the Alliance patrols in our sector? We're supposed to be protected."

"Look," said Kelly impatiently. "I can't help your people unless I get some answers. How many ships did they come with?"

"I don't know." Hamar looked almost sullen. "Enough cargo carriers to take our entire stockpile."

"Any fighters?" persisted Kelly.

"No. Yes. I'm tired," said Hamar, rubbing his face.

Kelly's exasperation faded. "I know you are," he said gently. "But it's important."

"There was a cruiser that fired on us. We were nearly killed. Some of my crew were blown out into space when the hull broke. Horrible."

"How did you get aboard this freighter, Hamar?" asked Kelly. "How did you get away?"

Hamar buried his face in his hands and didn't answer.

Beaulieu came up behind Kelly. ‘‘Enough questions for now,’’ she said. ‘‘Hamar needs rest.’’

‘‘Yes, I know,’’ said Kelly in frustration. ‘‘But there isn’t time to wait. Please, Hamar. It might help us when we get there.’’

Hamar looked at him in surprise. ‘‘But you know what they’ll do. Everyone still on Chealda will be killed when the Salukans are finished with them. We are all that’s left.’’

‘‘Maybe we can stop that from happening,’’ said Kelly. He glanced at Beaulieu. ‘‘Have you about got everyone squared away here?’’

She nodded. ‘‘We’ve distributed plenty of rations, providing they are careful.’’

Hamar glanced worriedly from Beaulieu to Kelly. ‘‘Aren’t you going to take us onto your ship?’’

‘‘I’m afraid we don’t have room for all of you,’’ said Kelly with a smile. ‘‘But we’ve got you rigged with enough heat and light to last you until the rescue ship comes.’’

Hamar’s thin hand closed over Kelly’s forearm. ‘‘You can’t leave us here!’’

His voice rose an octave. Seeing the frantic protest in Hamar’s eyes, Kelly pulled free and patted him on the shoulder. ‘‘Easy, my friend. You’ll all be quite safe. It won’t take long for someone to get—’’

‘‘No!’’ said Hamar, struggling to throw off his blanket. His mug crashed on the floor, splashing coffee. ‘‘You must stay with us. We’ll die here.’’

‘‘Nonsense,’’ said Beaulieu crisply. ‘‘No one is going to die. A Boxcan civilian ship answered our call and is diverting course to pick you up. She’ll be here within twenty-four hours.’’

‘‘You can stay with us until she comes,’’ said Hamar. ‘‘That’s not long. You said so yourself.’’

‘‘You don’t need us now,’’ said Kelly.

‘‘Yes, we do! We do!’’

Hamar’s shouting had disturbed the others. Kelly grabbed him by the arm.

‘‘Look, Hamar, get a grip on yourself. Panicking won’t do anyone any good.’’

Hamar was breathing hard. He clung to Kelly. ‘‘You must stay. You must!’’

"If we stay with you, we can't go to Chealda. We've got to try to save the others—"

"Can't," panted Hamar.

Kelly glanced at Beaulieu and nodded. She pulled out a tranquilizer patch, but Hamar saw her. He twisted away from Kelly and nearly stumbled. Kelly reached out to catch him and found himself staring into the business end of a small, snub-nosed nuker, the kind that did nasty things to neurons. Kelly froze.

Hamar glanced behind him. "Lupe! Kort! Take them!"

"What the . . . ," said Caesar.

Kelly glanced over his shoulder in time to see two of the refugees corner Caesar, Phila, and Baker across the lounge. Kelly swore to himself. Until Hamar pulled out the nuker, he'd thought the Chealdan was simply suffering from mild hysteria. Now he realized they'd been enticed into a trap.

Kelly glared at Hamar. "You'd better have a good reason for this, mister."

Hamar was shaking, but a nuker didn't require precise aim. "They knew," he said raggedly, "that the company would investigate our lapse in communications. They sent us out here to intercept—"

"Why?" exploded Kelly. "Hamar, we're here to help you. You can't—"

Beaulieu touched Kelly's arm. She was eyeing Hamar critically. "Conditioned—"

"No," said Hamar, shaking his head. "Not conditioned. We have our orders. No investigations."

"You can't hold us here indefinitely," said Kelly. "Another ship is coming."

"Hold you. Kill you. The next ship, the same," said Hamar. His eyes held a mixture of misery, shame, and determination.

"Why are you doing this? If they're holding someone close to you, coercing you—"

"No," whispered Hamar. He held up his free hand, baring the inside of his emaciated wrist to show an intricate blue mark. "I wear his seal. He let us go in exchange for this. He let us go! Don't you understand what that means? The Salukans never spare prisoners, but they let us go."

"You don't have to honor that deal," said Kelly. "Hamar, you're free now. You aren't under obligation to them—"

"You don't understand," whispered Hamar. His eyes widened and they stared through Kelly. He lifted the nuker.

Kelly launched himself at the old man in a flying tackle, praying he was below the nuker's line of fire. The weapon discharged with a sizzling blat, and Beaulieu screamed in pain. By then, Kelly and Hamar were struggling on the floor.

Hamar was stronger than he should have been, considering his age and condition. He writhed and squirmed beneath Kelly like something demented, trying with all his might to use the nuker. But Kelly's hand was clamped on his wrist and he strained to hold it pointed away.

He didn't want to hurt the old man, and that hampered him. Hamar kneed him in the stomach, driving out his air with a whoosh. Kelly doubled, and his grip slackened on Hamar's wrist. Hamar rolled out from beneath Kelly and scrambled away. Wheezing for breath, his face white and drawn tight, he gripped the nuker with both hands, aiming it at Kelly.

Desperately, Kelly kicked out, knocking the weapon up just as it blasted. The nuker went flying, and with a hoarse cry Hamar scrambled after it. Kelly skidded around on his hands and knees to Beaulieu, who was gasping and writhing in pain. Kelly opened a comm link.

"Recall. Recall. This is Kelly. Emergency recall, broad dispersal!"

There wasn't time to hope Siggerson knew what he meant. The teleport was designed for quick pickup *if* Siggerson was alert enough to activate it.

Hamar picked up his nuker in the corner and turned with it. The weapon was strictly short-range, but Kelly wasn't precise on just how short and he didn't want to guess now.

"Siggerson!" he shouted. *"Come on . . ."*

The nothingness of the teleport caught him and seconds later he found himself kneeling on the platform beside Beaulieu. The platform beeped a warning, and he barely had time to scramble off, dragging Beaulieu with him, before Caesar and Mohatsa materialized. They hurried off, and Baker materialized, panting and wild-eyed with Mohatsa's weapon in his hand.

Siggerson came running into the bay. "Everyone back?" he asked excitedly. "My God, what a tremendous piece of engineering. Simultaneous pickup with flawless hold memory to materialize two at a time in strict sequential order. Marvelous! I wondered how it would work, especially when all of you insisted on being over there at the same time. How does it—"

"Siggerson," said Kelly in exasperation. "Shut up. Beaulieu's hurt. Anyone else?"

He glanced around swiftly, but they all shook their heads.

"Close," said Caesar, still panting.

"Too close," said Baker.

"How bad?" asked Phila, kneeling beside Beaulieu.

Beaulieu's dark face was a queer ashen brown. She was still gasping, and her eyes were squeezed tightly shut.

"I don't know," said Kelly worriedly. "Very close range. Let's get her to sickbay."

"I'll help you," said Caesar. "Take her feet."

Kelly was even more out of breath than Caesar. He moved gratefully to let Caesar take her shoulders.

"Siggerson," he said, wiping sweat from his eyes. "Get us out of here. Back on course to Chealda, maximum speed. Warn that Boxcan ship. I don't know what the Salukans did to those poor devils, but they'd better be handled carefully."

"Right." Siggerson nodded and disappeared.

"What about our equipment?" asked Baker. "We can't just leave it there."

Kelly looked at him. "Do you want to go back for it?"

"Uh . . ."

"Right," said Kelly. "We leave it. Come on, Caesar. Lift her gently."

Beaulieu moaned as they lifted her off the floor. Her eyes fluttered open and focused on Kelly's face.

"Not bad," she whispered. "Stop effect with . . ." Her head tipped back and she didn't finish.

"Oh, great," said Caesar in disgust. "She would pass out just before she tells us what to do."

"You freeze off the wounded area," said Phila, keeping up with them as they carried Beaulieu down the corridor and into the sickbay. "So the damage doesn't keep spreading. That's about all you can do."

They laid Beaulieu on one of the beds and rummaged frantically for the proper equipment. Kelly vowed they would all have sickbay drills from now on so they wouldn't be so damned helpless.

"How does a bitsy atom like you know so much about it?" asked Caesar, leaving all the storage lockers open behind him. "Nukers are illegal. Damned good thing, too. I came within a centimeter of ending my career back there."

"I just know, that's all. There!" said Phila, lunging over Kelly's shoulder to grab a blunt-ended object that looked vaguely like a pistol. She shoved it into Kelly's hands and ripped open the fastenings of Beaulieu's tunic. "Hold her still, Caesar. Here, Kelly. Her side. It's still small. Freeze the area good."

Kelly frowned at Beaulieu's abdomen. Her skin was smooth chocolate cream except for a fist-sized area between her ribs and hipbone. There, it was oddly wrinkled and discolored.

"If it gets to her organs, she's done for," said Phila. "Hurry!"

"You'll burn her skin with that thing, Boss," said Caesar, looking as pale green as the walls.

Phila snorted. "Better some burns than to have her guts eaten out."

She was right. Kelly swallowed, forcing himself to overcome his reluctance. He pressed the piece of equipment—wondering what the hell you called such a thing—to Beaulieu's side. She jerked and screamed. Kelly snatched the freezer back, his heart hammering.

"Hold her better!" said Phila to Caesar. He nodded and pressed Beaulieu's shoulders down.

Kelly thought he might be sick, but he refused to give in to his own weakness. Grimly he pressed again, holding the freezer to Beaulieu's skin despite her screams, until he had ringed off the damaged area. When he finished, sweat was running into his eyes. He took a step back, feeling oddly weak.

"We should have given her a painkiller first," he said, wiping his face.

Phila took the equipment from his hands and put it away.

She began closing storage lockers. "Now, yes," she said. "Before, there was not time."

"She looks awful," said Caesar. His voice was a shadow and he looked as bad as Kelly felt. "Do you think she's going to buy it?"

"No," said Phila with confidence. She opened Beaulieu's medikit and found one of the basic first-aid painkillers they all knew how to use. Patching it on, she watched a faint hint of color return to Beaulieu's unconscious face and nodded to herself. "She'll sleep now."

"Damned Salukan *scatsi*," muttered Caesar, wiping his mouth. "Inventing weapons like that."

"I'm glad you knew what to do," said Kelly to Phila and she gave him a smile that was half shy, half cocky.

"Yeah," said Caesar. "You must have played with nukers back home."

Phila stiffened. "My past and my home aren't for discussion. Keep it in mind, Samms."

She walked out, leaving Caesar and Kelly staring at each other.

"Touchy as a Boxcan," said Caesar.

"What did you expect? That was about as tactless as you can get." Kelly thought about adding to Phila's warning, but held it back. His operatives had to sort out their own working relationships without his interference. He sighed, feeling suddenly hungry and very, very tired.

"We'll get there in time, Boss. Don't look like that."

"Sure." Kelly glanced at Beaulieu and pulled a thin blanket over her. They were going up against a Salukan force of unknown size, without a medic. He should have left her on Station 4 awaiting the arrival of Harrier squad delta. He wished he shared more of Mohatsa's confidence about Beaulieu's condition. "Casualty number one."

"Don't think that way, Boss." Caesar clasped his shoulder and gave him a brief shake. "We're in the Hawks because we're tough as hell. We all know the risks and accept them. If you start worrying over us this way, you'll freeze up. You can't do that, Bryan. You just can't."

Kelly met his eyes. "I can't keep losing my people either."

"You won't. Your luck was always good before Dexos. It will be again." Caesar grinned. "Come on. Baker has a bottle of Othian ale hidden in his duffle. Let's talk him into sharing a glass. There'll be time enough to worry about Chealda when we get there."

4

The shock of the electric lash whistled across 41's naked back without warning, laying open his flesh with a crackling snap that echoed down the mine tunnel. For an instant 41 felt only the jolting force of the blow, then the fierce sting of the cut took his breath. He straightened as far as the tunnel ceiling would allow and turned on the overseer with a snarl.

The lash struck again, sizzling a cut across his chest and driving him back a step. He mastered his anger, knowing that as long as the shackle remained on his ankle he was helpless. The faint stench of scorched flesh filled the hot, dusty air.

The overseer laughed, showing a pale gleam of pointed teeth in the shadows. "Better!" he said in the gutteral Saluk tongue. "You begin to learn, barbarian. This," he shook his whip with its barbed metal tip in 41's face, "is your teacher. Eh!" And he laughed again.

Abruptly he switched off power and hooked his whip around 41's neck. He tugged. "Kneel!"

41 went down on his knees in the rocks, wincing. He'd been here a week, longer than some survived in the mines, and his clothing of tough synthetic trousers, tunic, and soft boots of lyx hide was just about gone to tatters.

A draft blew through the tunnel, and he shivered. He reached for what was left of his tunic and shrugged it on over his sweaty skin. Blood oozing from his fresh cuts stuck to the cloth.

The overseer twisted his whip tighter about 41's neck. "That's right. We're moving you. Be still now. Keyman!"

A slim youth in a work apron and cloth tied over his hair

to protect it from the incessant dust came running. He bent beside 41 to unlock the shackle chain from the bolt ring, and while he struggled with the stiff lock his eyes slid to 41's face. 41 bared his teeth, and the youth flinched, jumping back and flinging the chain at 41 in a fury.

"Foreign dog!" he shouted. "Keep your distance."

The overseer tugged, and 41 got to his feet. "Come on. Tunnel eight for you."

"Good," said the keyman, licking his thin lips. Sweat and dust had blurred his eyepaint and created marks of their own. "That's the end of you soon. Good riddance!"

The overseer shoved 41. "Move, barbarian."

41 stumbled along the uneven floor of the tunnel. His night vision was far superior to the Salukans' but he was very tired and becoming weak from the lack of sufficient food and infrequent rest periods. The end of the chain lay cold and heavy in his hand. His long fingers tightened on the links. He was tempted to attack, but the whip remained twisted about his throat and the overseer carried a blaster on his belt.

Tunnel eight was at the lowest level of this mine. They took a shaft lift down into oppressive darkness broken only occasionally by an inadequate light glowing at each tunnel landing. At the bottom of the shaft, the lift thumped to a halt, jarring 41.

"I hate it down here," muttered the keyman.

The overseer laughed. "No one asked you. Off."

The keyman rolled back the wire door, and 41 was pushed off the lift and down a tunnel smaller than any he'd worked in before. Intense heat rolled over him. Fresh sweat broke out along 41's hairline and trickled down his temples. Ahead of him glowed a light, and he could hear the uneven whir and chink as ore was hewn from the walls.

Perhaps a dozen workers stood in place. Their faces ghostly white with dust, they paused to watch him pass.

"Food," murmured one weakly, reaching out.

The whip fell away from 41's neck and whistled out. The woman fell with a cry.

"Get back to work!" shouted the overseer. "No food for two more hours. Get to work, or I'll flay your miserable hides."

He lashed two more with electricity to emphasize his point,

then whirled on 41, who had not moved. "Very good," he said. "You're getting smarter. Keyman, put his ring bolt here."

The keyman crouched, bringing his tools from the capacious pockets of his apron. In swift order, he had welded on a new length of chain and ring bolt. 41 dropped his shackle chain on the ground as he'd been taught, and with a nervous glare the keyman swiftly passed it through the ring and secured the lock.

41 crouched upon the ground and began to gingerly ease off his tunic. He was at the foremost tip of the tunnel, which sloped to a dead end perhaps five feet ahead of him. The pick waiting for him was a heavy-duty model, fitted with a larger water line and stronger looking drill. He blew dust off the old goggles and slung them around his neck.

His back had begun to hurt quite a bit now that sweat trickled into the new cuts. The heat made him thirsty, but a glance at the waterbag told him it had been empty for a while. He felt suddenly flushed and weak. Wearily he rubbed his forehead. He had to hang on, he told himself. His chance would come, provided he kept watching for it.

The overseer gestured, and 41 lifted the pick and began shaking free the lines. He took his time, however, and as soon as the overseer and keyman had left, he lowered the pick and sat down to rest.

A little shower of rubble rained down upon his shoulder. "Sorry," said the woman chained next to him. "You'd better move, you know. They'll check your quota in two hours, and it had better be full."

She spoke in cultured Glish, the language of Earth. Her dust-coated hair was cut in a no-nonsense style that curled back from her temples. He paid little attention to human faces as a rule, but her eyes caught his notice. Gray, spaced wide apart, they were direct, remarkably clear eyes. Suffering and fear lay in their depths, but she did not look as though she shared the desperation of the others.

"I know," he said, answering in Glish. Street Glish, but she could understand it. Her brows went up, and he added, "I just finished a shift. I need to rest for a few minutes."

She stared at him for a moment. "You're here for punishment then?"

The question surprised him. "What else? Aren't you?"

"No, I'm—" She broke off with a slight frown. "Tosh, down at the other end, is here for punishment too. We get a few every week."

He blinked. "How long have you been in this tunnel?"

"Two weeks. Before then, I . . . Why? What have I said?"

He was inexplicably shamed. This small woman who came only to his shoulder spoke of weeks in this place of hell as casually as she might discuss a stay at a resort. Whereas, he was already wondering when he might die.

"We're scientists here, most of us," she said. "I can't pretend I am used to this kind of work, but I do know how to cut samples. You can't hack at it with brute strength alone. Or perhaps you can," she added with a quick glance at his muscles.

"I'm no miner," he said shortly. "Do you know the layout of these tunnels?"

"In general, yes. Why?"

"No overseer stays with you?"

"One comes by every two hours, and you'd better have your work done by then."

He decided he had nothing to lose by trusting her. "That's less supervision than I've ever had." He reached for his pick and shook out the water lines.

She frowned at him in dawning alarm. "Wait just a minute. If you're going to try a breakout, I don't—"

"You know the way out. You're coming."

"No! I—"

The rest of her protest was drowned out as he put the bit to the bolt of his shackle. He shattered it with one quick burst of power. Shards of metal exploded, some of them slicing through the top of his boot to his ankle. The pain made him suck in his breath, but he kicked off the fragments of the shackle with satisfaction.

"You're crazy!" said the woman, eyes wide.

The others stopped working and stared at him. Baring his teeth, 41 stepped toward the woman.

"Your turn."

"No!" she said. She lifted her own pick to hold him at bay. "I'm not getting my leg sliced off, thank you!"

His eyes met her alarmed ones. "Do you want to die down here? Or do you want to live?"

"I intend to do as I'm told and stay out of trouble until rescue comes," she said, backing from his approach.

"Rescue," he said in contempt, shaking his head. "There is no rescue except what you do for yourself."

"You're free," she said. "Go on and run for it. Leave me alone."

"No."

At the end of the line, the man she'd called Tosh shattered his shackle with his pick. But as the metal split, the bit slipped and dug into his ankle, grinding away bone and flesh before he could shut it off. His scream pierced the air, and he fell writhing to the ground.

The others stared at him in shock. The wet smell of blood filled the air. 41 took advantage of the woman's frozen horror to pin her against the wall with his shoulder and hip.

"No!" she screamed, struggling. "For God's sake, please don't—"

41 clamped his free hand over her mouth and stared intently into her panic-stricken eyes. "Do not move," he said.

She seemed to realize that he could not be dissuaded. She drew in a ragged breath and held it, her body stiff and motionless beneath his. He concentrated on placing the bit at the correct angle. One swift squeeze of power, and her shackle broke. She flinched with a little cry, but it was over. He released her and she stared at her ankle in wonder.

"I'm not even bleeding," she said.

He tossed down the pick and took her arm. "Come. There isn't much time."

She needed no urging now, but as they started down the tunnel, one of the other workers moved into their path with a rattle of his chain.

"What about us?"

"Yes," said the cringing woman whom the overseer had struck earlier for asking about food. "Please help us. Set us free."

41 kept going. "You can free yourselves."

"It's not that easy. Look at Tosh."

The gray-eyed woman knelt by Tosh, who was lying quietly now as his blood continued to pump out. His open eyes were glazing over, but they held such mute agony it was as though he spoke aloud. The gray-eyed woman touched his face gently, then glanced up at 41.

It was not necessary for her to speak. 41 knew what she wanted. He bent over Tosh, cradling the man's head in his hands. One swift thrust, and there was a loud snap of the fifth vertebra in Tosh's neck.

The gray-eyed woman shuddered, averting her gaze. 41 touched her shoulder and rose to his feet.

''Come.''

''Wait! Help us! Please wait!'' the others shouted after them. ''Kevalyn, you cold-hearted bitch—''

''I'm sorry,'' called back the gray-eyed woman as 41 took her arm again to pull her along. ''Please. Won't you help them?''

41 met her gaze briefly and shook his head. ''They are your friends?''

''Colleagues. Scientists like myself, most of them. We're from the research lab at Caru.''

The name meant nothing to him. He pushed her to the lip of the tunnel where it connected with the shaft. ''They are too many. They are too loud. Which way?''

''Up, of course. The lift—''

He tightened his grip on her arm. ''Don't be a fool. If it comes down, we are caught. There are other ways to get through a mine. You know them, or said you did. Which way?''

''All right,'' she said, expelling her breath. ''There are small, connective tunnels. Not all of them go through. But—''

''Good enough.'' He glanced about through the gloom and found a metal ladder bolted to the rockface of the shaft. ''Up that?''

''Where?'' she squinted, trying to see. ''We've got to have a torch.''

Despite the excellence of his night vision, he knew she was right. He glanced around in search of an emergency box and spotted it at the foot of the ladder. Limping to it, he found it locked. Seizing a chunk of rock, he smashed the clasp. He raised the lid and drew out a torch, a coiled length of thin, extremely strong rope, a first-aid kit, and a package of rations. It was all he could do not to tear open the latter, but he swallowed his saliva and handed everything except the torch to Kevalyn.

"Come," he said over his shoulder. He put his foot on the first rung of the ladder and started up. "We must hurry and get hidden far from here."

From inside the tunnel came the sound of a pick breaking a shackle. A cheer went up, and 41 scowled. They were noisy fools.

"Someone's free," said Kevalyn. "Shouldn't we wait—"

"No. Come."

He started up the ladder as quickly as his tired arms could pull him, but Kevalyn did not follow.

"I don't have to come with you."

"That is true," he said, panting lightly. "But I have the torch and the best chance of escaping."

"Why?"

He glanced down at her. "Because I am a hunter."

To his exasperation she still hesitated. "You'll get lost without me."

He bared his teeth. "I'll take that chance."

There was a moment of silence, then he heard the soft metallic echo of her feet upon the ladder. 41 smiled to himself and continued.

The climb seemed interminable. The muscles in his back and shoulders burned. Sweat poured into his eyes. Weariness washed over him, and he began to wonder if they would have to climb all the way to tunnel seven when he came even with a hole bored into the rock. It was perhaps a meter in diameter and had the smooth perfection of machine work. Without hesitation, he swung himself inside and waited for Kevalyn to join him.

It was hard for her. She struggled, unable to find the strength to step from the ladder into the tunnel. Finally 41 had to reach out and help her. He grunted as he took her weight. She scrambled frantically, clinging to his neck.

"You're inside," he said. "You're safe."

It took a moment for her to let go. Then she moved away hastily and crouched down. He could hear her shortness of breath.

"I'm blind in here," she said at last. "Aren't you going to switch on the torch?"

"Not while the light can be seen from the shaft."

"We should chance it," she said. "I'm not very keen on crawling around in pitch blackness."

"Give me the rope," said 41.

She passed it over. "You're going to tie us together?"

"Yes." He knotted it swiftly about his waist, then handed the other end to her. "I do not fear this tunnel. It is machine made, not natural. There should not be any bottomless pits to fall into."

"You're right," she said. Her voice was muffled while she fumbled to knot the rope. "I just don't like the dark."

"How far should I go? Is this simply parallel to the ore tunnels or does it—"

"There should be small connecting shafts. This is an inspection tunnel, put in when they were deciding how to best get at the veins. I think the shafts are about a mile apart. Sorry, that's the wrong measurement for you—"

"I understand the length of a mile," he said stiffly.

"You speak Glish very well."

She was trying to apologize and patronize him at the same time. She might as well have patted him on the head as she spoke. He frowned in the darkness and started crawling forward without another word. When the rope tugged tight between them, she followed.

His knees soon began to ache, then to hurt with an agony that flared up his thigh each time he put his knee to the ground. He tried getting to his feet instead, but he had to crouch so tightly the muscles in his back and buttocks screamed in protest. The tunnel was simply too small for him. He forced himself to keep going, not asking how Kevalyn was doing. The tug on his waist was steady, cutting into the soft part of his abdomen in a way that sometimes distracted him from the greater pain in his knees. He had chosen well with her. She could think for herself, and she had courage. He had seen it in her eyes from the first.

Half a mile into the tunnel, he gave out. He sank down belly flat on the round with a soft groan. Every muscle in his body burned. He switched on the torch for Kevalyn's benefit and closed his eyes, letting himself sink into the stone beneath him.

He meant only to rest, but he must have fallen asleep for

he awakened with a start, groggy and disoriented. The smell of food filled his nostrils. With difficulty he levered himself up on one elbow and saw Kevalyn sitting cross-legged behind him with the food package open.

Her gray eyes were luminous in the soft clear torchlight. "I'm glad you stopped," she said. "My knees were killing me."

41 smiled. "Mine too."

She smiled back, and it transformed the serious cast of her face.

"Your back is still bleeding, and some of those old cuts look half-infected. Do you want the first-aid kit?"

"Not now," he said, wiping all expression from his face. Being human she was probably unaware that she could not tend the hurts of a man who was not hers. "I want food."

Kevalyn shook out the ration bars in their foil packaging. "There were six, but I've already eaten one." She handed him three of the bars.

He unwrapped the first and started munching. It was tasteless and dry, reawakening his tremendous thirst. But he was too ravenous to care. When he started on the second bar, Kevalyn protested.

"Aren't you going to conserve those? It may be a long time until the next meal."

41 stared at her without comprehension. "Better to eat all of it now."

"But then you won't have any."

He shrugged. "I will hunt again when it's time."

Kevalyn stared at her two remaining bars for a while. He thought she was going to unwrap one, but finally she stowed both of them away in her pockets. He did not understand her wish to deprive herself, but it was her choice.

When he finished eating he felt stronger. "They will know soon that we are gone."

"If they don't already."

"We must plan," he said. "We must take the unexpected way out of this mine."

She smiled ruefully at him and shook her head. "There's only one exit."

He frowned, thinking that over. It did not look good, but he might be able to . . .

"You really are determined to escape, aren't you?" she said.

"Do you want to die down in this hole?" he retorted.

"No." She smiled and held out her hand. "I'm Kevalyn Miscetti."

Handshakes were a peculiar human custom. The Old Ones had taught him to avoid them lest part of his soul be captured by a witch; Harva Opie had taught him to avoid them lest he be distracted enough to get himself shot. Kevalyn was no danger to him, but 41 made no move to take her hand.

After a moment, she reddened and dropped her hand. "So you don't like handshakes," she said. "Do you have a name?"

"No."

A flash of anger entered her eyes. "Okay, fine. You don't trust me. I don't trust you."

She misunderstood, but he respected her temper. "You may call me 41," he said.

Her brows drew together, but after a moment she nodded. "All right." She sounded puzzled. "It's as good a name as any."

"It is not a name. It is a number. I have lost my name twice. I no longer use one. What I do not have cannot be taken from me again."

"But that's dreadful! How could your name be taken from you? I don't understand—"

"This gets us nowhere," he interrupted. "I had hoped there would be another way out besides the main shaft. A Boxcan told me once that on his world the mines are connected by cross cuts as long as twenty kilometers."

"Yes," she said doubtfully. "But those are for equipment transfers."

"How?" he asked.

"Rapid shot-tubes."

"Big enough for us to fit inside?"

She stared at him. "You can't be serious! It's too dangerous—"

He gripped her shoulder. "Don't be a fool. Every moment of life is a risk. Only death is safe. Now, quickly, Kevalyn. Tell me how we get to one of these cross cuts. We will be hunted soon, and they will think of these connection tunnels.

Even if they blow gas through here, it will be enough to finish us.''

''All right!'' She drew a shuddering breath. ''I'll tell you. But you have to agree to something first.''

''I don't make deals—''

''You will this time.'' Her gray eyes looked both scared and determined. They didn't waver from his face as she said, ''I know where the nearest cross cut is, and I know how to program the shot to stop in the correct mine. Do you?''

He glared at her, but she had him and they both knew it. ''What do you want done? Don't ask me to go back for those fools.''

''You aren't a Satter employee, are you? You must be off a supply ship or—''

''What has this to do with anything?' he said impatiently.

''Just that you don't know what the Salukans are doing here.''

''Stealing pyrillium. You waste time.''

''No.'' She gripped his bare arm. ''When they came in, they blasted our communications satellite. But if one of us could get to the comm center in Caru Refinery, a call could be made on the emergency transmitter. It will take a long time without the satellite booster on the signal, but in a few weeks it will reach one of the fleet patrols.''

''A few weeks,'' he said scornfully, shaking his head. ''That does not concern me.''

''But don't you see? They've baited a trap. Hamar and a few others were conditioned and placed on a damaged freighter. Anyone who picks them up will be misled into—''

''No,'' he said. ''There is me. Only me. As long as you help me in escaping, there is you. That is all, Kevalyn. Others do not matter.''

''But they must!'' she said urgently. ''41, if we don't do something the Salukans will kill everyone when they leave. Surely you have heard of their atrocities.''

''That's why I want to escape.''

''We must all escape!'' she said.

''You have madness. Why not ask me to blow up the whole refinery while I am there?''

''I've talked to people down here in the mine,'' she said, ignoring his sarcasm. ''Caru, Kuupke, and Harch have all been taken. But the northern settlement hasn't been touched, as far as I can tell. I can go there and connect with Dr. Rege Miramon's anthropological team. If I can help organize a resistance, then we have a chance to survive."

Hearing the fervor in her voice, 41 considered reminding her that all the Salukans had to do was pinpoint each settlement on this planet with the battlecruiser's sensors and blast them out of existence.

"Will you go to Caru for me?" she asked. "Will you help us drive out the Salukans? If we all work together, we can come up with a way—"

"How?" he countered. "Drive them out with sticks and snowballs?"

"We can break into the armory. We can fight, if we have the chance. Will you—"

"Why isn't survival enough for you?" he asked.

She stared at him. "Because the Salukans are robbers and murderers. Look how many have died in this mine alone. They've broken treaties and violated every convention between the Alliance and their empire. They've robbed this world of a year's income. They intend to leave without a trace, with all of us dead and no indication that a Salukan was ever here. We mustn't let them get away with it."

He still thought her crazy. "What happened to waiting for rescue?"

She flushed. "I had some time to think while we were crawling through the dark. It seemed that since you gave me this chance I should use it to its fullest extent."

"Most people think only of themselves."

Her gaze shifted away from his. She loosened the knot at her waist, then retied it. "Just say my social conscience has something to do with my family and the way I was raised. That's the deal, 41. Take it, or we split ways here."

He bared his teeth at that little threat. "And if I leave you here, what will happen to your plans of revenge?"

"This time *I* have the torch," she said softly and smiled.

Angrily he sprang at her, making her cry out as he knocked her sprawling. He plucked the torch from her grasp, making the light swing wildly, and scrambled back from her. They glared at each other in silence, then he unknotted the rope from his waist and let it fall.

Her eyes widened and seemed to shimmer in the light. She said nothing, however. Only the expression on her face betrayed her.

She was beautiful and beseeching. She had honor, even if that was something better possessed by fools. He found his anger dying.

"I will go to Caru," he said.

Relief lit up her face. "Thank you. I—"

He had to turn away. Inside, a voice mocked him: *She'll get you killed. You learned long ago never to serve an idealist.*

But his hands went on coiling the thin rope. Without looking at her again, he said, "We have rested long enough. Let us hurry and go."

5

The shot-tube operated on some principle of magnetics and compressed air. Kevalyn explained it to him while he dragged the dead Salukan trooper out of sight around a jagged outcropping of rock. Busy stripping off the trooper's buff-colored imperial uniform, 41 paid her no attention. As long as machines could be used, he did not care what made them work.

The trooper was close enough to his height for the leggings and tunic to fit. He found the uniform scratchy and smelling too much of perfumed oils beneath the dust imbedded in the fibers. Fitting on the sash with the crest of the pharaon emblazoned in gold and crimson threads, he strapped on the heavy belt with its blaster and ceremonial dagger. Then he pulled off the trooper's coarse black wig and leather cheek straps and did his best to cram his shoulder-length mane of blond hair under it.

When he emerged into the dimly lit tube landing, Kevalyn looked around and gasped.

"It's perfect," she said. "No one will question that you're not one of them."

He frowned and strode over to the opened shot. Peering down into it, he said, "Is this ready?"

"Yes, I've programmed it, and the tube is clear. The shot moves approximately sixty-four kph on straight sections and it isn't designed for hu—I mean, people as cargo."

He looked at her beneath the straight bangs of the wig. "I am human," he said.

Her expression flattened into a polite neutrality that meant she didn't believe him but wasn't going to say so. She nodded. "Of course. Anyway, it won't be comfortable."

"That does not matter."

He climbed into the shot and folded his legs up so that he could fit into it on his back. There was barely room; the top of his head jammed against metal. He grimaced to himself, then shut off the uneasy twist of his nerves. Anything to get out of here, he told himself.

Kevalyn stared down at him. "You don't have any phobias about being enclosed in small spaces, I hope."

Despite himself, memories of sitting in the dark tomb of an Old One came to him. Memories of days spent in a crate awaiting transference to the slaver who bought his childhood. Memories of icy nights huddled with the others in the tiny living cells of Colony 5-Alta, which had no atmosphere and precious little dirt to grow salm.

"No phobias," said 41, meeting her eyes.

She nodded. "Good luck, 41. I hope to see you again."

He did not believe in luck, and he did not think their paths would ever recross. With nothing to say, he reached up for the hatch. She shut it for him, blocking out all light with a suddenness that was unsettling. There was no internal latch; they had agreed to risk using the shot without the outer locks fastened down. Drawing in a deep breath, 41 tried to steel himself for takeoff.

Nothing, however, prepared him for the sudden swoop of velocity that squashed him against one end of the shot. Acceleration was almost instantaneous. He swallowed grimly and held onto consciousness against the g-force. It felt as though the bones in his face were being squashed flat, and he fought not to panic. The ride was as rough as Kevalyn had warned him; he seemed to feel every jolt and rattle as the shot hurtled and twisted its way along the cross cut tube. The song of steel against steel rang in his ears.

He tried not to think about the fact that he could not get out of this thing until it stopped. There really wasn't enough air. Already he had to fight for each breath. Soon he was so jolted and numbed he could not think. All he could do was close his mind to fear and endure.

* * *

The stop was so sudden it brought a grunt of pain from him. It took a moment to rouse himself from his stupor. He waited cautiously until he was sure his journey was over. Then he pressed his palms against the hatch, lifting slowly despite the urge to fling it open.

No trooper stood guard on this landing. Groaning under his breath, 41 maneuvered his stiff body from the shot and hobbled across the landing. It took awhile to work the kinks from his back and legs. But as soon as he could straighten enough to copy the arrogant swagger of a trooper, he stepped onto the lift and let it carry him up out of the ground.

The overcast sky brooded pewter dark, and wind stung his face as he stepped outside for the first time in eight days. He drank in the cold, clean air like freedom.

The refinery complex sprawled in an ugly collection of vast stinking tanks, mismatched buildings, porta-huts of corrugated stylene, sheds like peaked hats over rumbling generators, pipes snaking from building to building, many parked earthmovers and ore carriers painted a garish orange, and living quarters rowed up like barracks, all confined within a three-meter-high fence of electrified wire. Frozen snow drifted along the rutted ground. Salukan boots crunched in quick cadence as troopers marched from the barracks to a waiting transport. Another transport came rolling in to unload dusty, disheveled troopers coming off guard duty in the mines.

Salukan officers in their crimson sashes and heavy cloaks swore and shouted, directing a ponderous line of ore carriers past the refinery onto a frozen, unpaved road that curved northeast into the barren foothills ringed about Caru. Just over the top of the ridges could be seen a pillar of smoke. That would be the smelter, 41 decided. If the Salukans still had it running, maybe they weren't going to leave Chealda after all. Now that they were here, having such success at raping it of the ore, perhaps they meant to claim it permanently.

If so, he had *no* chance of getting off this frozen rock. His ship had been confiscated. He could continue to pass himself off as a trooper, but the thought of becoming one of them made his gorge rise. Kevalyn was right about doing something to shake the Salukans off this world. Otherwise, the rest of his life he would be chained here, and he could not bear that.

It had better be done quickly before he was spotted by an officer.

He set off across the busy complex at a purposeful pace, saluting officers whether they glanced at him or not. It would not do to wander, nor could he ask directions. He studied the buildings from beneath the bangs of his wig and gambled on a central one that was three stories and stood above the rest of the complex.

His guess was right. Inside, he found himself confronted by an expanse of data banks which apparently monitored every mine on the continent. Some Salukans stood about, but most of the actual workers were company employees with Satter emblazoned on the back of their thermal coveralls.

A guard blocked his path. "You have business here, trooper?"

41 stared into those dark purple eyes with black notched deep into the pupils. For a moment his mind was blank. The guard frowned, and his bronze-colored skin darkened across the cheekbones.

"If you've come in here just to get warm, you'll have demerits on your—"

"No," said 41 hastily, using the harshest Saluk negative.

The guard blinked, and 41 dared not let this moment of opportunity slip away from him.

"The communications," he said. "At once. I carry a message for—"

"Ah," said the guard, stepping back with a nod. "Minlord Chumiri is upstairs. Come, I will escort you to him."

The guard turned and strode across the room to a metal staircase. 41, cursing to himself, had no choice but to follow. The last thing he wanted was to cross paths with a minlord. 41 covered the butt of his blaster with his wrist. Maybe he could shoot him. That would throw the Salukans into an uproar and perhaps give Kevalyn her chance.

It would also get him gutted on the spot. He frowned.

"You look as though you've come straight from the mines," said the guard as he trotted up the steps ahead of 41. "Filthy place. I'm glad I haven't drawn that duty."

41 grunted. They reached the second floor, and he glanced along the featureless corridor.

"Not that way," said the guard. "Only the computer center and storage down at that end. Minlord Chumiri is in his office."

41 hesitated, but the guard was staring at him. He swallowed hard, feeling his muscles tensing too tight, and turned left toward the closed door where two burly guards in the tunics and leggings of private livery stood at attention.

"Message for the minlord," said the guard and jerked his head at 41.

The coldest, most suspicious pair of eyes 41 had ever seen glanced his way. "From the mines?"

41's mouth felt as though it had been stuffed with salt. He swallowed quickly, then still did not trust his voice and nodded without speaking.

"Peculiar," said the guard in livery. "Why not use the comm? What is this problem you bring the minlord, trooper?"

41 met his gaze and tried not to look nervous. "It is for the minlord's ears."

Both guards in livery frowned. "And perhaps you are an assassin from the fools who want to go home. Check him for hidden weapons!"

The man who'd brought him up here seized his arms and pinned them behind his back. 41 grimaced in pain. Dissension among the Salukan forces was something he understood. He could invent a tale for this, but let the ghosts of the Old Ones be merciful and allow him to find some means of getting out of here.

"None, other than these weapons on his belt."

41 was released. He took a step to one side and rubbed his wrists. The man who had brought him here was dismissed. One of the guards in livery knocked discreetly on the door.

After a moment it opened perhaps the width of a hand. Someone peered out. Murmurs were exchanged. The door shut. The guard glared at 41.

"You will wait."

41 nodded and leaned his shoulders against the wall opposite the minlord's door. After a few seconds, the guards quit staring at him. He gazed down the length of the corridor

where the comm center lay out of reach. If he ran, it would take at least eight seconds to get there. How long to establish a signal? He knew a few basics, but the whole center might be shut down. Then he would have risked his neck for nothing.

Well, he'd risked it already. He might as well finish the job.

And the only payment a woman's smile. 41 sighed. He was a fool.

His decision made, he delayed no longer. Drawing his blaster in a swift motion, he shot both guards in quick succession, giving neither a chance to return fire. The blaster was a clumsy weapon that kicked in his hand and was hard to aim. It also made a lot of noise.

He heard a shout from inside the room and the crash of overturned chairs. But 41 was already running, stretching out his strides and ignoring the pain jolting up his injured ankle. The corridor seemed endless. He'd never get to the end of it in time. Already he could hear the door opening behind him and a shout.

A shot would follow.

He passed a window that marked the midpoint of the corridor. 41 was tempted to dive out it and take his chances with the fall below. Better a broken leg than a shot in the back. But he kept running, dodging as he went.

The first shot missed wide. The second scorched his elbow. Crying out, he launched himself into a rolling dive on the floor and came up in a crouch that left him facing his opponents. He fired, and one of the aides in civilian clothes went down with a hoarse scream. The other ducked back into the minlord's office.

41 scrambled upright and ran on. Reinforcements were already pounding up the stairs. 41 knew he didn't have a chance. But he wrenched open the door and flung himself panting inside the comm center. His blaster was ready, but no one was working in here. He snapped on the weak lock that could be kicked open in a single blow and let himself sag there for a moment, trying to get his breath back.

The room was smaller than he expected, cramped even. It held a bewildering array of instrumentation and panels. 41 wiped the sweat from his face and began to study the boards as quickly as he could, refusing to let himself think of the seconds running out on him.

The boards were labeled. Each mine had its own comm link. Relief swept over him, and he found the controls marked TemStar ComSat. The satellite was out, but he could still send a message. But it wouldn't have the satellite boost behind it. At least that was Kevalyn's theory. He hesitated over the controls, however, cursing his own ignorance. There wasn't anything complicated about this. A child could activate this board. *Think,* he told himself. *Think!*

Flipping the upper right-hand toggles, he let out his breath as a hum answered. The board lit, and a message ready signal came up on the small screen.

Behind him a thud rattled the door. Startled, 41 whirled, his mouth dry, his heartbeat going like thunder. The thud came again, cracking the cheap stylene panels of the door. 41 fought the urge to crouch and open fire. He could hold them off until he exhausted his blaster charge. Then they would take him, and nothing would be accomplished except a few dead Salukans. Better to send the message.

But there wasn't time. The door shattered into pieces. Someone shouted. Expecting searing agony between his shoulders at any time, 41 hurriedly typed in "SOS" and keyed for repeat/constant.

"You!" shouted a voice. "Get away from that board!"

41 didn't look up. He had to finish now. He still had to send. A blaster roared; it deafened him, and at the same time he felt a tremendous force hit his left side. It spun him, and he saved himself from falling by clinging to the board. He felt nothing yet, only a numb paralysis in his side and arm. Sometimes it took you that way. Sometimes your nerves got crisped so instantly they couldn't send the pain message up to your brain. You could die and not even know it.

He hit the necessary switches, concentrating on getting the sequence right. It was simple, yet the world seemed to be fading on him. His knees buckled, and he struggled to hang on, just hang on one more second to hit that final control.

Hands grabbed him, but they were too late. His fingers scrabbled desperately and pulled. A red light flashed "SENDING" and he wanted to laugh in triumph. But all he could do was fight for breath because his lungs seemed to be locking up.

They dragged him away, shouting and pummeling him with angry fists. An aide in an intricately woven tunic of bright blue, mauve, and silver tried to cancel the message. But he couldn't.

He whirled on 41, his young painted face livid with rage. "What did you do, traitor? What did you do?"

A shudder passed through 41. He was sinking, although the guards still held him up. So simple, really. Kevalyn had told him to key in CONSTANT. The message would recycle indefinitely on its weak little signal length unless power to the whole refinery were cut.

Groggily 41 realized the aide was shouting at him again.

"Can't stop it," said 41. His voice sounded thick and far away. His heart was jerking oddly, struggling to live while the rest of him faded out.

"You fool," the aide said. "You've done this for nothing. It won't get anywhere. Not even to the outer edge of the atmosphere."

41 stared at his painted face that elongated, then broadened, then blurred altogether. Along with vision went cognizance. All he could hear was his own voice say faintly, "She asked for it, and it was done."

He was glad his last act had not been done for money. And after that, there was nothing at all but a deep, black silence.

Sleet fell from an iron-gray sky, rattling upon the snow-crusted ground. Wind blew steadily, sweeping the gaunt sides of a series of ridges broken from the foothills of a mountain range lost in cloud. A narrow valley carved out by an ancient river long since dead sheltered a shallow lake coated in ice. Dead shrubbery rattled in the wind.

Kelly teleported into the valley, materializing in the open about a half-meter from the lake. That was just a little too close to getting wet for comfort. He scuttled into the bushes for cover. His breath fogged about his face, and the cold penetrated through the thin thermosuit worn under his uniform. He rubbed his bare hands together, longing for gloves, and unslung his diehard.

His fingers moved deftly, twisting the release catches that

telescoped out the muzzle and hollow stock. He locked them into place, checked the sight to be sure it was focusing properly, and switched on the internal circuits so they'd be good and warm if he needed to fire.

The process took twelve seconds. Shivering, Kelly opened hailing frequencies on his wristband communicator.

"Kelly to ship," he said softly, keeping a wary lookout in all directions. "Down and ready."

"Acknowledged." Siggerson's voice faded in the distortion caused by the scrambler. They didn't want the Salukans picking up their signals. It had been tricky enough establishing a geosynchronous orbit without detection, but the *Valiant* was well hidden now behind her waver shield. "Compass dispersal of teleport continuing."

"Right," said Kelly. "Any variance in that beacon signal?"

"Negative."

"Any response?"

"Negative."

Kelly frowned. It didn't look good, that tiny SOS pip coming out of the center of the Salukan HQ. After the last trap, with those starving refugees as bait, Kelly worried that this might be another. But why? He shook his head. Second-guessing a Salukan was next to impossible. They were born devious. All he could do was hope the SOS came from a resistance group.

"Keep sharp," he said. "I'll check in every thirty minutes."

Warily he left concealment and headed north. As he climbed the first ridge, puffing for air that cut his lungs, he kept watch for any airsled patrols. At the top of the ridge, he paused briefly for a survey with his binocs. He could see the unpaved road winding up through the mountain pass from the refinery. Heavy machinery crawled along it.

Kelly's mouth set itself in a grim line. Hamar, however else they'd gotten to him, hadn't lied when he said the Salukans were mining raw ore in addition to the stockpiles they'd already stolen. Did they honestly think the Alliance would let them get away with this?

Stowing the binocs, Kelly hurried down the other side of the ridge. Ice patches made his footing tricky. He crouched low, sliding down the steepest parts with a clatter of dislodged shale and frozen ice.

The sleet came down harder, stinging his face and hands. He squinted, quickening his pace in order to keep warm. Caesar, Phila, and Baker were supposed to be closing in on the complex from the three other directions, doing a sort of manual search and check as they went. Normally they would have used hand scanners for the job—those hand scanners which Caesar hadn't gotten aboard. Without them, they were half-blind out here. Looking at the bleak landscape that seemed devoid of any life, Kelly doubted they would be lucky enough to stumble across any of the Satter employees.

At the top of the next ridge he could see the smokestacks of the Caru Refinery. Crouching behind a leafless thornbush, Kelly programmed his binocs for maximum magnification. The buildings leaped at him.

Homely, utilitarian, the refinery sprawled out from the base of the foothills. Row after row of storage tanks fashioned from rusting metal and linked by catwalks blocked much of his view. None of the stacks belched fire, but the place teemed with activity. He estimated perhaps a full legion of troopers in the distinctive gold and tan imperial uniforms. Kelly smiled ruefully to himself. Four against a hundred.

He switched his wrist comm to local frequency and double-checked the scrambler. "Kelly here. Everyone in place?"

"Yo, Boss," answered Caesar cheerfully. "Is hell this cold?"

"What have you seen?"

"I'm near the road. Five heavy ore carriers have gone by. The last load of the day, judging by how much time we have before nightfall. Plus two transports of troopers followed them as far as the refinery junction before turning off. Guards for the miners, I'd guess."

Kelly grunted and lifted his binocs to his eyes again. "Yes, I see them. New detachments are getting on to go back."

"There's computer activity," said Phila. Her voice faded in and out through the scrambler. "But not full capacity. From the oscillation patterns, I'd say they're just operating the monitors. No data input or dumps going on. I've pinpointed the beacon in that tall building."

"Good work," said Kelly. He switched frequencies. "*Valiant*, come in."

"Siggerson here." The pilot's voice remained as dry and unruffled as ever.

"Send down that short cannon to Samms. He'll give you his current coordinates in a minute."

There was a pause. "Kelly," began Siggerson doubtfully. "Are you forgetting that battlecruiser up here?"

Kelly frowned. "What about her? Has she picked you up?"

"No. But she *will* hunt us, as soon as you start fireworks planetside. She could ram us inadvertently and if I have to move, we'll lose the waver. I thought you were going down for a looksee."

"Losing your nerve, Siggie!" called out Caesar.

Siggerson did not reply. Kelly was all too aware of how Siggerson stood between them and being stranded down here. "Get off, Samms," he said angrily. "Siggerson, we're going to cause as much trouble as we can. Your job is to keep the *Valiant* from being detected. Now send down that cannon."

"Last chance to play hero, eh, Kelly?" said Siggerson.

Kelly flushed hot. He lowered his wrist and glared across the snowswept hills until he had his temper back under control. "Samms, where do you want to set up?"

"I need to be about a hundred meters closer, Boss," said Caesar. "And the higher, the better. If the shots are dropping from a high trajectory, they'll have more trouble pinpointing the source. I'd like to start with some delay bombs and scatter them. Then bring on the heavy stuff."

"Not too heavy," warned Kelly. "Remember the civilians. Wipe the barracks first."

"Yo, Boss. Can do."

"And stay away from that central building. The research facilities are probably there." Kelly shivered and shifted position to take the wind from his face. "Phila, I want you and Baker to deploy Klopers along that road. Cut the complex off from the mine and the smelter."

"Right, Commander," said Phila.

Kelly paused. "Baker? Do you read me? Baker?"

Several seconds went by before Baker's voice, slow and insolent, came over. "Yeah, I read. I was just wondering what you're going to be doing while we're out here playing hero.''

Anger swept through Kelly, but before he could respond Caesar was saying hotly, ''Kicking your butt to Andromeda, brig bilge. You—''

''That's enough, Caesar,'' said Kelly. ''Everyone to your positions. Signal in when you're ready. Wait for my word.''

They acknowledged, and Kelly started down the last ridge on his belly. He'd sat too long in the cold without moving. He was chilled now, and his muscles had started to stiffen. But moving soon limbered him up again.

He dropped into a gully and flattened himself. The fence enclosing the complex stood less than twenty meters distant. He heard the slow crunch of footsteps and dared peer over the lip of the gully. A sentry, head bowed against the lash of the wind, tramped past. He was drawn with cold, and sleet glittered on his black wig. Kelly hesitated, tempted to take him since he wasn't the least bit alert. But Kelly needed to know how frequently sentries came by this point so he waited, clenching his jaws to keep his teeth from chattering.

Fifteen minutes passed and every one of them seemed an eternity. Nearly frozen, Kelly roused himself at the steady crunch of footsteps. It was the same sentry, still dragging along with his shoulders hunched and his hands rammed into his armpits. His weapon hung slackly off one shoulder.

Kelly grinned to himself and snaked up and out of the gulley as soon as the sentry passed from sight. Kelly unsnapped his clippers off his belt and checked their reverse charge to be sure it was working. Carefully, he cut himself a hole in the wire, grimacing as sparks snapped and crackled about his hands. Dealing with electrified wire was always tricky. The antiquated stuff could fry a man in seconds, and colonists preferred it because it was cheaper than forcefields. But he couldn't have gone through a forcefield without shutting down the whole barrier.

By the time the sentry returned, Kelly was inside the compound and waiting. He leaped out of hiding and tackled the Salukan, careful not to roll toward the fence. The sentry might not have been good at his job, but he was big and hard to pin down. Kelly's first chop at the back of the Salukan's neck bounced off, deflected by the thick fibers of his wig.

The sentry turned under Kelly, twisting onto his back. He reached for Kelly's throat, but Kelly sent the stock of his diehard thudding into the man's jaw. The Salukan went limp, and Kelly dragged him swiftly out of sight behind a pile of rusting barrels.

Panting, Kelly wiped the sweat from his face and headed along the perimeter of the fence at a run, keeping well to cover. Whoever ran the refinery had a poor eye for security. Barrels, cast-off equipment, and sheds had been allowed to stack up against the fence in order to expand room in the center of the complex. That made it easy to keep out of sight.

As he went, Kelly kept mental track of the passing minutes, aware that his people had had time by now to get into position. He paused behind a corrugated porta-shed and activated his wristband.

"Kelly to—"

Shouting and general commotion made him break off. He pressed his back to the shed and eased to the corner. Peering around it, he saw a knot of troopers escorting a lone figure through the complex. The prisoner had his hands clasped on top of his head. He wore a dark uniform.

Kelly squinted, not wanting to trust his eyes. Mouthing a curse, he pulled out his binocs and let autofocus do the work. It was Baker.

Stunned, Kelly lowered the binocs a moment and tried to figure out what could have possibly gone wrong. He looked for more prisoners and saw only Baker. Had a foot patrol spotted him on the road?

A tiny electrical nudge from the inside of his wristband notified him that someone was calling. Whipping back out of sight, Kelly brought his wristband up to his mouth.

"Kelly here," he said softly.

"Caesar here. Checking in."

"Mohatsa. I'm ready."

"Stand by," said Kelly. "They've caught Baker."

"What?"

Both of them tried to speak at once.

"Can it," said Kelly. "I'm down here in the compound. I'll get closer and see what I can do."

"Watch yourself, Boss."

"Yeah," said Kelly grimly. "You two keep sharp. At my signal, let loose with all you've got."

Cutting off, he moved positions, paralleling Baker's progress as best he could. But ahead stood a crudely constructed sentry's box, marking the end of the route for the sentry he had taken out. Kelly veered off sharply, darting from cover to cover. He was unhappily aware of the catwalks overhead from which he might be spotted at any time. So far, there didn't seem to be anyone up there. But he couldn't trust to luck forever.

The troopers with Baker stopped in an area between the administrative buildings and an open lot of parked earthmoving equipment. Panting lightly so that his breath steamed about his face, Kelly edged closer. He huddled first behind a fuel tank, then scuttled behind a parked loader.

"Hey, don't shove!" said Baker. "I keep telling you. Friend. I'm a friend. I got information to sell. You just take me to your leader. Understand? L-e-a-d-e-r. Don't any of you wig-heads speak Glish?"

Kelly drew back, feeling as though he'd been kicked in the solar plexus. For a moment he simply couldn't believe it, then rage swept him. He wanted to mow down Baker and the rest of them with his diehard. Of all the *stupid* treachery. . . .

"Glish?" said a staccato voice, heavily accented. "Yes? You have something to say?"

Kelly mastered his fury enough to glance past the tank again. He saw an officer in a heavy tan-colored cloak standing before Baker. Baker answered too quietly for Kelly to hear, but it wasn't necessary to listen to what he said. What mattered was that he not tell the Salukans anything that could blow this job.

Kelly bowed his head. He didn't want to do this, hated Baker for making him do this. Angrily he tapped his comm.

"Caesar. Phila," he said quickly. "You have go light. I repeat . . . you have go light."

"What?" asked Caesar. "Are you out? Did you get him?"

"Never mind that. Do it *now*!"

"Yes, sir," said Phila.

"Boss," said Caesar. "What the hell are you doing? If I start raining bombs down on you—"

"I'll look out for myself," said Kelly. "Hurry!"

Caesar said nothing. Frustrated, Kelly watched the officer laugh and gesture for the troopers to take Baker inside. Baker was a fool; the Salukans would drain him dry of every scrap of information he had and then kill him. It happened to spies and defectors all the time.

A Space Hawk had never turned before. It made Kelly sick just to watch Baker. He thought of the incalculable damage. Methods used by Special Operations, codes, equipment design . . . all that and more could go spilling into the intelligence files of the enemy.

But not this time.

Kelly switched to the ship frequency. He'd have Siggerson yank Baker out now.

"Kelly to *Valiant*," he said urgently. "Siggerson, come in. We need emergency teleport."

No answer.

Kelly stared at his wristband. There wasn't a malfunction. The receptor worked perfectly. But Siggerson didn't come back to him.

He tried again, refusing to believe the most likely explanation. "Kelly to Siggerson. Come in, damn you! Siggerson!"

Nothing. Not even static. Just the smooth silence of no transmission.

He pushed emergency recall, hoping to operate the teleport's standby system from here.

It didn't work.

Kelly lowered his arm, feeling suffocated. The *Valiant* was gone. Whether she'd been blown out of orbit or she'd fled made no difference. He and the others had no way out now. No safety net. No teleport to yank them if things got too hot.

Meanwhile, the troopers were escorting Baker away.

Kelly jumped to his feet and aimed his diehard at Baker's back. He wasn't going to let it happen. Even if it meant killing one of his own men.

The sights blurred. He realized his hands were shaking. *Damn you, Baker,* he thought and squeezed the trigger.

6

He missed.

In the last possible split second, Kelly knew that he couldn't kill Baker, especially not by a shot in the back. Baker had to stand the trial he deserved. Even if Kelly had to drag him out of the complex and force him to live on roots and berries for the next fifty years until rescue came, he'd do it.

Kelly's hands jerked, and the plasma bolt hit the trooper standing next to Baker. He fell with a scream, and the Salukans whirled in confusion. Orders rapped out, and two troopers headed toward Kelly's hiding place.

The advantage of surprise was gone. Kelly climbed into the seat of the loader, crouching as low behind the controls as he could. They didn't provide much cover. He hit the firing button, and the engine coughed to life with a deafening splutter and roar. Smoke belched out the exhaust. Kelly wrapped his free hand around the cold metal shift. He threw it into gear, and the loader shuddered forward.

A whine past his ear pinged into a metal cross-strut directly behind his seat. Kelly crouched lower and began firing back, his diehard kicking as he braced the stock in the hollow of his hip and steered erratically with his other hand. A ground-floor window in the central building slagged, and Kelly swore at himself. If he kept shooting that wildly, he might as well go home.

The Salukan officer seized Baker by the arm and dragged him into a run, heading toward the administration building. Kelly veered the loader after them, skipping a gear and making the engine scream as it revved too fast.

Overhead, a flat pop left a smoke trail in the air. Then there came a whole series of pops. Kelly smelled the acrid discharge as the smoke trails interwove and faded. Caesar's scatter charges were in place. Kelly saw one of the white packets drift and flutter to the ground like a worthless piece of debris. Frantically Kelly steered around it.

Doing so cost him valuable time. The officer ran up the steps and shoved Baker into the building. Kelly fired on the doorway after them in sheer frustration.

In the distance, Phila's Kloper blew up the road with a roar that shook the complex and sent a crimson fireball rolling into the sky. Salukans not already alerted by the sound of shots now boiled out in all directions, gesturing and shouting.

The loader's treads hit the steps of the building and ground away with a horrible grating of metal over stone. Kelly left it struggling there and jumped down. A shot ripped through the seat he vacated.

Startled, Kelly dropped to his knees and slid around as close to the cover of the grinding treads as he could get. The angle of that shot told him a sniper had him sighted from one of the catwalks.

There. Between two storage tanks.

Kelly brought up his diehard and focused the sights on long-range. He fired, and the sniper fell. But another shot ripped his sleeve, and Kelly dived for the door in a frantic roll and kick. The door slammed open, and Kelly scuttled inside with a burst of fire squeezed off for cover.

He slagged two valuable-looking pressure gauge monitors and set off fire claxons. A computer overloaded, and smoke began pouring out its circuit panels. But the workers had already been cleared, and no one waited in here to ambush him.

Cautiously Kelly lifted himself off the floor and looked around the cluttered area of work tables stacked with equipment, scales, ore samples, and computer disks. At one end of the room stood a metal staircase.

"Damn," breathed Kelly aloud.

At this point he could still back out and escape with reasonable odds of getting out of the complex. If he went up those stairs, his chances plummeted to zero. But he'd never backed away from a challenge, and he wasn't going to do so now. With the *Valiant* already compromised, there was no going back anyway. Besides, he wanted to get his hands on one of those perfumed Salukan officers and choke the whereabouts of Kevalyn out of him.

He started for the stairs.

From outside came the scream of artillery, followed by an explosion that rocked the building. Kelly nodded to himself in satisfaction. Caesar had cranked up the shot cannon at last. In minutes he would start activating the scatter charges now littering the ground of the complex. The safest place to be, for the moment, was right here inside this building.

Kelly had reached the stairs when the sound of gunfire above him made him crouch for cover. What the hell were they shooting at up there? He was the only active assault member in the complex.

Unless some of the miners were fighting back.

Kelly took the stairs two at a time, his diehard aimed and ready at his hip, his heart hammering like thunder. Another shell screamed outside, close enough to make his nerves scream with it. The explosion shattered the windows on the landing, and Kelly ducked beneath a shower of glass.

That involuntary crouch was the only thing that saved him from a plasma bolt. It lanced over his head and sent chunks of wall flying. Kelly dropped flat and scrambled, his mouth dry with fear. He managed to get out of the limited line of fire before the next bolt came. The glass on the floor slagged together in a puddle and lay steaming in the cold air.

Kelly caught his breath and lifted his head during the pause. His ears were ringing, and blood trickled down his cheek from a cut. He touched it gingerly and managed to smear blood across his face.

Stalemate. His opponent with the cheap diehard clone could squat up there ahead of him on the stairs all day and pick him off the first time he tried to move. And he couldn't lie here pressed against the banister forever. The first batch of troopers who ran inside this building to take cover from the shelling would have him trapped.

"Well?" demanded a voice in harsh Saluk.

"I hear nothing. I think he is dead."

"Go and see."

Kelly mouthed a curse. Two of them. That made it even worse. One would flush him out for the other to pick off.

He was lying on his gun arm. Slowly, trying to make no sound, he rolled farther onto his back to free it and brought up his diehard. As he listened to the trooper easing his way cautiously down to the landing, Kelly drew out his prong and opened all three blades.

There came the crunch of a foot upon glass. Kelly could hear the trooper's breathing, hear him trying to be stealthy. Kelly tensed, then forced his muscles to relax. His fingers tightened on the hilt.

The trooper was good at this. He eased around the turn of the stairs onto the landing with sinuous caution, keeping most of his body behind the scant cover of the newel post as long as possible. Kelly lay motionless, barely daring to breathe. He could smell unguents and stale beer on the other man—that peculiar mixture of odors that was so repulsively, characteristically Salukan.

"Eh," said the trooper with sudden confidence. *"Il vasweem esce murthet."*

He stood up and stepped toward Kelly, who threw the prong. It caught the trooper fairly low in the chest, right above his heart. The trooper loosed a strangled grunt and doubled over, falling in a crashing roll down the stairs past Kelly.

The other Salukan let out a shout of surprise, but he was too smart to investigate. Swearing, Kelly hauled himself to his feet and made the turn up the landing. He expected to get the top of his head blasted. But all he caught was a glimpse of the officer, running.

Kelly went after him, stumbled, and reached the top of the stairs on his knees. He shot while he was still sliding and managed to wing the officer in the leg. The Salukan fell sprawling, but shot back. He was using a hand blaster—the kind that had a lot of force at close range, but not much accuracy otherwise. The shot missed Kelly, who was already running forward.

The officer stared at him in horror, and screamed as another shell went off outside. The scatter charges were exploding now across the compound, lifting black smoke into the air and confusing the troopers scurrying for cover. All the windows along the corridor blew out with a concussion that slammed Kelly into the wall.

Stunned, he tried to keep moving, but for a moment he was groggy and wobbling. The officer aimed his blaster, but missed again. Kelly swung his diehard like a bat and knocked the blaster flying.

The officer pulled himself to a sitting position. His copper-skinned face was drawn with pain and fear. His black eyes darted from Kelly to the windows and back again.

Kelly aimed the diehard right at his face, knowing that to the Salukan the muzzle looked as huge as a cannon. "Now," he said, panting. "You've got a certain member of my squad. I'd like him back."

At the end of the corridor, a door opened and three troopers appeared. One of them held a flame-thrower that could incinerate Kelly where he stood. He stared, unmoving, knowing from the hollow pit that suddenly formed in his stomach that he didn't have a chance of getting out of this now.

"Barbarian," said a harsh, heavily accented voice from behind him.

Kelly turned and saw the tall officer who had taken Baker coming from the other end of the corridor. The tan cloak had been flung back over his shoulders, revealing folds of crimson lining. This officer walked toward Kelly. He held a blaster aimed at Kelly's midsection.

"Surrender your weapon to Oparch Nisis." His Glish was gutteral but fluent. As he drew closer, Kelly saw that his lean bronzed face was seamed by age and weather. His wig shone blue-black with the luster of silk fibers and fell upon his shoulders in long thin plaits. A magnificent ring flashed upon the hand that held the blaster.

Kelly swallowed, running quickly through his options. He could make a break for it and die now, or he could do as he was told and die later. He switched off the charge to his diehard and handed it to the wounded oparch on the floor.

The richly clad officer looked past Kelly and gestured. The troopers approached, two of them holding their weapons trained on Kelly while the third one searched him.

Don't panic, Kelly told himself. Caesar and Phila were still out there loose. All he had to do was somehow get word to them.

''*Comme qu'sce thet, vasweem.* Hand over your communicator.''

In spite of himself, Kelly moved in protest. Swifter than thought a rifle butt crashed against his temple. Consciousness blinked out on him, then cleared back. Gasping, he found himself on his knees. Pain throbbed through his head. The troopers unfastened his wristband and jerked it off.

The Salukan who was obviously in command stepped close enough for the long hem of his embroidered tunic to brush Kelly's face. He curled his fingers in Kelly's hair and tipped back Kelly's head.

Kelly grunted in pain. Purple eyes glittered down at him. They held no mercy. The Salukan put away his blaster and drew his ceremonial dagger instead. He held the curved sharp blade against Kelly's exposed throat.

''Barbarian,'' he said harshly. *''Ta esce murthet. Maitan!''*

''Minlord!'' A man came running down the corridor. ''Minlord Chumiri! Bad news from the ship—''

Chumiri released Kelly and turned. ''What has happened?''

''The carrier's payload doors malfunctioned, and she dropped everything. The entire cargo is floating in space.''

''What?'' Chumiri's weathered face flushed dark bronze. He brandished his dagger at the messenger, who blanched.

''The report just came, minlord. I—''

Another explosion outside shook the walls. Chumiri swore upon the full panoply of Salukan gods.

Kelly, who'd managed to recover his breath by this time, sent him a mocking smile. ''Having a bad day, minlord?''

Chumiri struck him with the back of his hand, sending Kelly sprawling into the wall with enough force to knock the wind from his lungs. He wheezed, doubling up.

''That one,'' said Chumiri in imperious Saluk. ''Put him with the other. We'll have their execution as soon as the fighting is over.''

In spite of the cold that numbed his face and fingers, Caesar was sweating as he swiveled the short cannon on its specially designed grav-flat. He dropped in a fresh charge, swore as the hot metal side of the cannon burned his palm, and thrust down the anchor bolt to stabilize the grav-flat for firing. Three charges to go—including the one he was about to fire—then he'd be out of ammo.

Using his binocs, he sighted his next target in the gutted complex now swept with smoke, fire, and debris. An hour left until nightfall, and he had a lot of work to do. As soon as he finished here, he was to call Siggerson for pick up and set up a firing site at the smelter. Phila had already blasted a crater in the road with a good solid bang of her Kloper that made his heart swell with admiration for a job well done.

Dropping the binocs, he did the calculations in his head and tapped in the new trajectory. His fingers felt like wood. They were red and swollen, and they hurt. Hoping Kelly wasn't anywhere near the fuel tanks, he hit the firing button. The short cannon barked with a diffusion of smoke back in his face. Its recoil rattled against the anchor bolt and sent a tiny avalanche of loose shale and gravel rolling down the hillside.

In the complex, the fuel tanks blew in multiple succession, sending huge fireballs roaring into the sky. He could almost feel the heat at this distance. Caesar grinned to himself. When he finished, that complex was going to be as flat as his first wife's chest.

The cannon steamed in the cold air. Caesar blew it a kiss and unlocked the anchor bolt. "Good baby," he said. "Spin for Daddy."

Something cold and metallic touched the back of his neck, sending a small shock through him. He reached reflexively for his diehard.

"Don't move," said a voice in Saluk.

Caesar froze, his eyes widening. Yusus, he thought in disgust. He'd been too caught up in what he was doing to watch his back. A green recruit would have known better.

The weapon jabbed him in the neck, and a foot stamped in the center of his back, forcing him down on his belly in the snow. The foot stayed on him while a second Salukan searched him. His precious new gel packets and a couple of DeFlex grenades were plucked out with grunts of interest. His wristband came off next. Caesar hoped the search would stop there, but it didn't. The Salukan found his prong in its hidden pocket just above the inside of Caesar's knee. Caesar closed his eyes.

The foot left his back. "Up!"

Caesar didn't move. "Aw, hell. Just go ahead and get it over with. Don't make cat meat out of me."

A kick in his kidney left him gasping and dizzy.

"Up!"

Caesar staggered up to his feet and turned slowly to face his captors. They were Salukans all right—with lean faces no wider than his hand and dark eyes so close together they might as well have looked out the same hole. Mean devils, every one of them. They probably wanted to scare him some before they killed him.

He cocked his head and pushed himself up on his toes a little to make himself look taller. His heart might be going too fast and his palms slick with sweat, but he wasn't going to let a pair of clowns in eyepaint get to him.

Besides, he had one thing left that they'd missed. A circlet of braided clear filament was fastened around his right wrist with an oblong bead of gold. It was almost invisible and to a casual glance seemed nothing more than a plain sort of ornament.

But it contained a miniature launcher inside the bead, with a maximum range of two meters. The launcher carried microfilament with a strength of eighty pounds per inch. It wasn't the line, however, that interested Caesar, but the velocity of the launcher itself. He eyed the explosives the shorter of the Salukans cradled awkwardly in his hand. If he could hit that DeFlex just right, he might manage to detonate it.

"There are more of you," said the tall Salukan, speaking Glish through a translator slung about his neck. "How many?"

Caesar rocked higher on his toes. "About forty."

The Salukan scowled. "You lie."

"If you know the answer, what are you asking me for?" retorted Caesar. He took a half step toward Shorty and rubbed his left wrist. "Yusus, you boys going to take me to your leader, or what?"

The two Salukans glanced at each other, puzzling through his words. Caesar edged a little closer. He wanted to be near enough for a good hit, yet if he got too close, he'd be chopped liver along with them.

"We will take you nowhere," said the tall one finally. He

lifted his long-range rifle. ''We have all of your weapons. How many more of you are there? Answer, and we will kill you quickly.''

''Thanks,'' muttered Caesar. ''That really makes it worthwhile.''

Deciding he had to take the chance now, he stopped rubbing his wrist and lowered his hands to waist level. Flipping his right wrist up, he pressed the bead and prayed his aim hadn't gotten too rusty in the few months since he'd used this thing.

The tall Salukan was motioning with his weapon. ''You will turn around—''

He never finished his sentence. The launcher hit the top of the DeFlex grenade, and the result was a contained blast that blew the world apart. Blinded and deafened, Caesar was flung back as though shoved by a gigantic hand. Maybe he was flying. Maybe he was flying in pieces. Maybe he'd just keep on going and never come down.

Cartwheeling, he hit the ground with an impact that jolted the fuzzy bits of his consciousness back together. He went rolling down the hillside, and rocks and dirt from the blast came down with him. The frozen ground and gravel seemed to be peeling off bits of him as he went, but he had no more than the dimmest awareness of what was happening. And in his mind he could see Kelly's chiseled face, those steely blue eyes smiling at him from beneath straight dark brows. And Kelly was saying, ''Kind of a drastic way to make a break for it, don't you think?''

''Yo, Boss,'' Caesar muttered.

He slid to the bottom of the hill and lay there in a heap, half buried in dirty snow and shale. And when the blinding dazzlement behind his eyeballs finally faded, he still didn't know how many bits of him were doing a fallout over the countryside.

Phila knelt in her hiding place approximately forty meters from the crater that had once been the road to the smelter. She didn't glance down at the destruction she'd caused. The twisted hulks of metal and sprawled bodies made her faintly sick to her stomach. Nothing in training simulation had prepared her for the actual result of what some of these weapons could do.

Not that this was the first time she'd ever seen a dead man. If she were that green, she'd never have been admitted to the Space Hawks. Still . . .

Don't think about it, she told herself, busy telescoping the broad barrel of the Kloper down into its case. She fastened the strap and slung the thing over her shoulder.

"Mohatsa to *Valiant,*" she said. "Come on, Siggerson. I need pickup."

Nothing.

She frowned and swiftly checked her wristband to see if it could be malfunctioning. The way the snow had started to fall here, maybe moisture had gotten into the casing. But she could find nothing wrong. And the commander had called her just a few minutes ago.

A shell whistled overhead. She watched it go, bursting over the refinery with a spray of smaller firebursts. Caesar was doing the best artillery job she'd ever seen. Pride surged up in her throat, and she was glad she'd joined the Space Hawks, glad she served with Kelly. And that made her doubly determined to do her job and Baker's too.

She called the *Valiant* again. "Siggerson, come in. I need recall now."

Nothing.

She switched off in frustration. "Damned *cosquenti* civilian!"

If Siggerson had lost his nerve and abandoned the mission, then she prayed to live long enough to hunt him down for it no matter where in the galaxy he might hide.

But there was still the other road to blow up. If she couldn't teleport there, she had to find another way.

Phila gazed down at the wreckage below her. Not all the ore carriers had been caught in the blast. The last one in the convoy had only plowed into the side of the hill bordering the curve in the road. She picked up her diehard and made her way swiftly down the hill.

The snow blew harder, and she felt cold despite the double layer of thermals beneath her uniform. Her ears and fingers hurt the most of all. She couldn't feel her toes inside her boots. But that didn't keep her from running across the open space of the road to the cab of the carrier.

The few survivors stood about in a daze, and the one who drew a weapon on her got cut down by a quick plasma bolt. Phila climbed the ladder bolted to the cab and thrust the muzzle of her diehard through the window at the bleeding driver. He wasn't Salukan.

For a moment they stared at each other. Phila recovered first. "Can you drive?" she asked.

He was holding his hand pressed against his temple where blood trickled freely. "Yeah," he mumbled. "Think so. Where did you come from?"

"I'll tell you on the way," said Phila, climbing inside. The cab towered above the ground, giving her an excellent vantage point. "Back this thing up. I want to blow up the road on the other side of the refinery."

He studied her. "Between Caru and Long Sally Mine?"

"If that's what you call it. Yes." Impatiently she gestured. "Come on, mister. Move this thing. I got work to do."

He grinned and fired the engine, which belched to life. The whole carrier vibrated. Slowly, ponderously the treads gripped and slipped and gripped until it backed away.

Phila watched alertly for any stray troopers who might try to stop them. "Is there any wide spot where we can turn around, or will you have to back the whole way down?"

"Little lady, I can drive this carrier frontwards and backwards. I can take her anywhere you want to go."

Another shell screamed overhead. The driver glanced that way and scowled. "You people sure are welcome. We been in a fix here with these goons taking over and stealing everything we got. I hope you blow every single one of the bastards to kingdom come, that's what I hope."

Phila met his eyes and nodded. Somehow it didn't seem fair to tell him that his rescue force consisted of herself, one man on artillery, a missing ship, a traitor, and a commander stranded under fire somewhere inside enemy lines.

Don't think about it, she told herself fiercely against the tight scared knot inside her stomach. *Just do your job.*

7

Siggerson felt a slight stir of excitement. It was working.

Humming to himself, he finished running the infiltration program that linked the *Valiant*'s computers to those of the Chealdan defense system. Contrary to what Hamar had told them, the Salukans did not destroy the satellites. It would have been very foolish of them, since the exponential factor of recoil would be hazardous for any ships in this solar system. Instead, the Salukans had simply used a sophisticated long-distance frequencer that shut off certain key functions. That shouldn't be possible, but since the Salukans had done it Siggerson didn't see why he couldn't reverse the process.

It was all a matter of tracing down the proper calculations. He'd tried to explain this to Kelly, but the commander had obviously not understood more than a tenth of what Siggerson was saying. Siggerson knew explosives and artillery had their place, but if he could reset the defense satellites, he could also tamper with the electrical systems of the two Salukan ships. With that accomplished, the Salukans would be trapped here on Chealda, and there was no need to risk the lives of the squad in a spectacular display of heroics. They could simply hold the Salukans here until the fleet arrived.

The data came spitting out across his screen. He hunched over it eagerly, doing mental tallies with previous figures.

"Do you want some food?" asked Beaulieu from behind him.

Smelling coffee, he frowned impatiently at the distraction. "No. I've got it. Finally. And no fluctuations in my readings this time either. Everything looks firm."

She took a station seat beside his. "I don't like it."

He sighed. They'd been through this before. "You're wasting my time."

"Voicing a justified opinion that happens to be contrary to yours is not wasting time," she snapped. "We are supposed to be maintaining constant readiness. If you start shutting down key systems such as the waver shield and teleport—"

"For only three-quarters of an hour," he said with as much patience as he could muster. "Why is it so difficult for you to conceive of the basic—"

She banged down her coffee cup. "It isn't difficult for me in the least. You forget that I am a scientist. The principle of your plan is brilliant. Your ability to do the necessary calculations is admirable. Is that sufficient praise? It's your sense of timing that's at fault."

"Why?"

"Why?" She glared at him. "Why can't you wait to execute this operation until Kelly and the others come back up?"

"And when will that be? They'll need time to set up their attack positions."

"Yes, and once the shooting starts, they need precise monitoring."

He scowled. "I *know* that. But—"

A little beep warned him that the infiltration program was loaded. He swung back to his instruments. It took scant seconds to tie in his commands.

"Siggerson, don't—"

"Executing now." As he spoke, he pushed the controls and his data board lit up with rapidly scrolling figures. The quarterdeck lights faded then came back up as power systems accounted for the momentary imbalance in drain.

"All you're doing is alerting that cruiser of our presence," said Beaulieu. "Kelly will have your hide for this."

Siggerson barely heard her. The program links were interfacing smoothly. He smiled. "Not if it works. Sit tight, Doctor, and watch this."

He switched on the main viewscreen and focused sensors on the satellite chain. "The second one from the left is the controller. If everything loads in correctly, it will rotate toward the sun."

A faint shudder ran through the *Valiant* as her automateds

tapped a pulse of energy from the battery reserves to correct gravity drag. That in turn caused a hiccup in the running program. Siggerson hovered over his boards, but nothing seemed to have gone amiss.

Then a warning sounded from the sensors. He shot out of his seat and went to that station for a complete status listing.

"What is it?" said Beaulieu. "I *warned* you—"

Siggerson brushed past her and returned to his master station. He brought in a view of the Salukan freighter. "Her payload doors malfunctioned. She's dropping her cargo."

Beaulieu swung around to stare at the viewscreen. "What caused that?"

"We did. Uh, I think we did. Look."

As he spoke, Siggerson watched the ore and oil barrels floating out into space. It looked like a massive garbage trail. Eventually it would string out into a rubble cloud junking up orbital paths. He might have to replot their own—

"Great. Just great." Beaulieu threw up her hands. "Why don't you just open a hailing frequency? We're supposed to be invisible—"

"Look at it," said Siggerson, smiling. "They'll never get it cleaned up. They probably don't have the equipment or the expertise."

At fifty kilometers off the freighter's port bow, the battlecruiser—an enormous A-shaped craft with a linking strut between her two implosion-drive wings—suddenly powered up and moved position. She wallowed ponderously at sublight speed, pulsing just enough to nudge herself out of the path of the debris.

Siggerson stared at her in fascination. She was huge; she was deadly; she was moving.

Beaulieu's hand closed on Siggerson's shoulder, making him jump. "Cut off that link."

"Three more minutes," he said, "and we'll have—"

"Cut it off now!"

A light flashed on the sensor board. Siggerson pulled himself erect in his seat and checked it. Beaulieu was right. The Salukan sensors had crossed theirs. They'd been located. He swore and cut the program link with two and a half minutes short of full implementation.

"Get communications and teleport back on," Beaulieu said. "We'll have to yank our people and get out of here."

Siggerson frowned. "Don't panic, Doctor."

She glared at him. "Urgency is in order, Mr. Siggerson. They know we're here. One shot across our bow and we're—"

The sensors told him that the Salukan cruiser was definitely moving around the planet toward them. Siggerson put all the systems on board the *Valiant* to complete on-line status. It would be close, but he loved to shave the smallest possible margin off anything he attempted.

"Contact the landing party," he said. "Coming to full power now. We'll be ready to exit orbit as soon as they come aboard."

Beaulieu snorted. 'Finally." She seated herself at the communications board and fumbled with the controls. "*Valiant* to Kelly. Come in, please. *Valiant* calling Kelly. Come in. Mohatsa, come in. Samms. Baker?"

Siggerson glanced at her with a frown. "What's wrong?" he said sharply. "Are you sending correctly?"

"Yes! No one answers."

Worry went through Siggerson. For the first time he realized that Beaulieu's protests might have been justified. He hesitated only a moment.

"Very well," he said. "We'll have to yank them. Get down to the teleport bay. I'll operate it from here."

Fuming, worried, Beaulieu left her seat without a word and climbed down to the lower deck. She tried running to the teleport bay, but that started a dull ache in her half-healed side. Slowing, she stopped off in sickbay long enough to grab her medikit. Siggerson was an idiot, an ivory tower pedant who couldn't see beyond his own interests. He'd put the ship and possibly the landing party in danger out of a disregard for anything except his own experiment.

She'd encountered plenty of research scientists with the same tendencies, but the greatest harm they ever did was to inject themselves with experimental serums that either killed them or won them scientific prizes and acclaim. Siggerson played with lives. The fool ought to be locked away.

The teleport bay was a cramped area in the rear of the ship where the rumble of the engines could be felt despite insulated bulkheads. Entering, she frowned at the narrow platform. Siggerson should have had them aboard by now. She touched the comm.

"Quarterdeck," she snapped. "What's the hold up?"

"No contact," he said. "Check to be sure their wristband codes are entered."

Frowning, she studied the controls and found what she needed. The board in front of her lit up in swift succession. Four codes registered. Only one indicated contact.

Swiftly she touched the recall control. At the same time she reactivated the comm. "Siggerson, you're not only careless, you're sloppy. I'm recalling one contact now. Stand by."

He started a question, but she cut him off. The teleport platform shimmered silver before her. Mohatsa materialized, holding her diehard in one hand and a grenade in the other.

For a split second they simply stared at each other in dawning horror. Then Mohatsa jumped off the platform, tossing down the grenade as she did so.

"Live!" she yelled. "Send it!"

Startled, Beaulieu slapped the wrong control and an error buzz sounded.

Mohatsa was already crossing the short distance from the platform to the controls like a whirlwind, brushing Beaulieu aside. Swiftly she hit reset and sent the grenade. Just as it dematerialized, a shudder went through the ship.

Siggerson signaled over the comm. "What the hell is going on? We just got our hull scorched by some kind of explosion."

Beaulieu and Mohatsa looked at each other in mute relief. Phila's hair was powdered with snow now melting into droplets that shimmered on her thick hair. Grime streaked her face, and one sleeve of her coveralls had been ripped from the wrist to the elbow.

"Hello?" said Siggerson's voice. "Respond, please."

Phila scowled and touched the comm. "You're damned right I'll respond. What's the idea, yanking me like that? You nearly got the guts blown out of this ship pulling that stupid stunt. Why didn't you call?"

"You didn't answer," said Beaulieu before Siggerson could. "We're in trouble. Siggerson has managed to give away our existence to that cruiser."

"What?" Phila stared at her. "Then we have to void this

mission. We can't outshoot that thing. Where're the commander and the others?''

Beaulieu shook her head. ''No contact.''

''But I thought the commander was back on board. He was bringing Baker up before Caesar started shelling.''

Beaulieu shook her head. Phila frowned. Worry filled her dark eyes.

''Then they're dead or in trouble. Let me check this out.'' She leaned her diehard against the console and bent over the controls.

Siggerson signaled again. ''The cruiser is on stat visual. We have to move position now—''

''No!'' said Beaulieu. ''We don't have the others.''

''We can't sit here waiting on them.''

Phila growled something rude under her breath. ''We find them now. You, Doctor. Are you fit?''

''Yes,'' said Beaulieu at once. She ignored the lingering twinge in her side. A few trifling aftereffects of the nuker could not be allowed to scrub her from what needed to be done. ''I'll get a weapon and warmer clothes—''

''No time,'' snapped Phila. ''Get the weapon. While you're at it, bring me four DeFlexes and some of Caesar's explosive gel. This teleport's still set on the original down coordinates. I'll recalculate. Move, please.''

''Right.''

Beaulieu hurried into the arsenal. She pulled out a diehard for herself and slung it over her shoulder, then hunted for the explosives Phila wanted. Filling her pockets, she hesitated then picked up one of the three-bladed stilettos which regulations specified she was to carry at all times. She also grabbed goggles, gloves, and a couple of food packets which shouldn't have been in here at all but which were lying on the floor as though they'd been dropped.

When she got back to the teleport, Phila already stood on the platform. Phila tossed her a wristband.

''Come on, Doctor. I've entered the code for you.''

Beaulieu juggled the stuff in her arms to fasten on the wristband. Stepping onto the platform, she said, ''But what about the ship and—''

A slight wave of nausea displaced her. Split seconds later, she materialized in the midst of a snowstorm blowing at perhaps five knots, with dusk obscuring the rough terrain about her and neither light nor sign of civilization in sight.

She took a step and stumbled, shivering already as the cold robbed her of breath. "Phila!"

"Here." Phila's hand gripped her arm from behind.

Beaulieu turned and thrust gloves and explosives at the tiny operative. The wind whipped through her ears, making them hurt. "We need shelter!" she shouted over the wind, pulling on her own gloves. "Hypothermia . . . danger!"

"Worse if it gets dark on us!" shouted Phila back. She unslung Beaulieu's diehard and opened out the stock and muzzle for her. "Here. Charge it immediately and stick close to me. We can't risk being separated."

Beaulieu nodded. "What about the ship?"

"To hell with Siggerson. Come on!"

Phila headed into the darkness at a run. Grimly Beaulieu forced herself to keep up in spite of the snow stinging her face. She thought of her university job conducting anatomy drills and how much she'd hated the quiet comfort and security. Right now it seemed a paradise.

Overhead, a light flashed through the dark clouds. Phila halted, and Beaulieu nearly bumped into her.

"The first torpedo," said Phila. "It missed, or it wouldn't be coming down into the atmosphere." She lifted her fist. "Outrun them, Siggerson!"

Beaulieu tapped her on the arm. "Keep moving," she said through chattering teeth. "We'll freeze soon. We must find shelter."

"We're a quarter mile from the complex. We can do it, Doc."

Beaulieu nodded, hiding her dismay. She kept thinking of things like frostbite and pneumonia. She also thought of Kelly and the others. "The Salukans don't take prisoners. Are we insane to be down here instead of running for it with Siggerson?"

"Yusus!" shouted Phila in disgust. "Hawks don't leave their own kind. If they're alive, we get them out. If they're dead, we blow these greasy wig-heads away."

She began to run again. Muffling a groan, Beaulieu followed.

* * *

Someone was making a lot of noise, enough to wake Kelly up. Irritated, he opened his eyes and realized that the noise-maker was him, groaning. He shut up and lifted a hand to his temple where his head throbbed steadily. His fingers touched crusted blood and a swollen lump that hurt. Kelly dropped his hand to his side and decided oblivion was the best place to be.

The shock of icy water thrown in his face sent him struggling to a sitting position. He gasped, freezing and wet, and focused reluctantly on two figures looming over him in the shadows of wherever he was.

The taller one grasped him by the front of his uniform and dragged him onto his feet. In the dim illumination cast by a low-wattage porta-lamp, Kelly saw a lean, bronzed face with chiseled, sloping bones and fierce amber eyes glowing out beneath the thick bangs of a black wig. The trooper topped Kelly's height by a couple of inches. He held his left arm cradled against his side as though he had been wounded.

Behind the trooper stood Baker, looking both apprehensive and insolent.

Kelly glared at him. "You yellow-backed coward! What the hell do you think you've gained by this?"

Baker stepped away from the trooper. "Plenty. I'm not dead, am I? No, I got me a way out of here."

"Have they questioned you yet?" said Kelly, barely able to contain his anger. "One session with their mind sieve and you won't—"

"That isn't going to happen to me," said Baker.

"Isn't it? What makes you think you'll be an exception?"

The trooper's grip loosened slightly. Kelly jerked free and glared at both of them. Belatedly he noticed the trooper wore no weapons. Kelly's gaze narrowed, and he glanced around at his surroundings.

They were spartan. The Salukans were using a porta-shed for a guardhouse. Unheated, its thin walls provided scant protection against the elements raging outside. Cracks where walls improperly joined the roof let icy drafts whistle through. Suppressing a shiver, Kelly returned his gaze to the trooper.

"*Hut,*" he said in the curt Saluk way of greeting. "Are you in here for dereliction of duty or to act as a spy?"

The trooper blinked. "Your Saluk is good," he replied in

the same language. "But why speak in the tongue of our enemies?" he added, switching to a version of the street Glish spoken on many of the colony worlds. He bent his head and pulled off the wig. Tangled blond hair spilled to his shoulders, and he tossed the wig into a corner.

Baker's mouth fell open. Kelly let a corner of his mouth curl into a smile.

"I see," he said, thinking this man must have Salukan blood somewhere in his ancestry. "Good disguise."

"Thanks." The amber eyes studied him frankly. "You wear the uniform of a Space Hawk. Legit?"

Kelly nodded. "You're a miner? One of the company employees?"

"No. I am a mercenary. I did some escort duty for an independent supply ship and got caught here."

Kelly studied him, making note of the slightly slouched, yet alert stance. He was lean, almost thin, but he looked quick in spite of his height. His lack of expression gave nothing of his inner thoughts away.

"Why are you wearing a Salukan uniform?"

The mercenary winced and supported his left arm. "It was a way to escape the mines."

"But you got caught."

"Yes." The mercenary frowned. "A woman in the mine with me asked me to do her a favor and set the distress beacon." He glanced at Kelly. "You came in response to it."

"We were already on our way, but, yes, we did pick up that signal," said Kelly. He smiled halfway. Ordinarily he had little use for mercenaries. They did more harm than good; most of them were little better than roving brigands. "Is that how you hurt your arm?"

"Yes. Baker says you have the fastest ship in the galaxy. It's equipped with a teleport, and all that's needed to gain access is to recover the wristband communicators. Is that true? If I help you escape, will you take me off this planet?"

Alarms went off in Kelly's head. His friendliness dried up. "No."

Anger flashed in the mercenary's eyes, but he muted it swiftly. Shrugging, he said, "Baker says there were four of you. Not many for an assault, but you did well. The complex is nearly flattened."

Ignoring the compliment, Kelly strode up to Baker in two swift steps and gripped him by the front of his uniform. ''Anything else you've blabbed, Baker?''

Baker knocked his hands away. ''Keep off me, Kelly! I'll say what I please to anyone I please.''

''You'll keep your mouth shut. You've jeopardized all of us, and I—''

''Me?'' Baker's eyes opened wide. ''You're the one with the reputation for getting your squads killed. Killer Kelly, that's you.''

Heat burned across Kelly's cheekbones. He stared at Baker, seeing the panic in Baker's eyes, in the tremble of his mouth. Baker was the dangerous kind of coward, the one who turned on his comrades if he felt cornered.

Reasoning told Kelly that, but underneath it the old twist of guilt came back. Kelly shook his head. ''My mistakes aren't the issue here—''

''They should be! You've treated us all like expendables. It ought to be you who's up for charges, not me.''

''That's enough, Baker.''

Baker clenched his fists. ''I'm not taking orders from you again. I got me a way out of this mess, and I'm taking it. Nothing you do is going to stop me, see?''

''And what about him?'' asked Kelly with a sweep of his hand to indicate the mercenary, who'd retreated a few paces to watch them. ''You idiot, you've handed him the *Valiant*, providing he can get one of the wristbands. Can't you think?''

''I . . .'' Baker frowned and glanced uncertainly at the mercenary. ''Yeah, but he—''

''Look,'' snapped Kelly, ''if you lost your nerve, that's one thing. But you risked everyone in the landing party by turning yourself in. Now you've blabbed your guts out to a complete stranger who looks half Salukan and could be a spy planted in here as a prisoner with us.''

Baker backed up a step. ''I'm not getting killed because of you, Kelly.''

Kelly grabbed him and shook him. ''We're all in this together! Samms and Mohatsa are still—''

''No, they aren't!'' shouted Baker, twisting free. ''They got Samms. How long do you think Mohatsa lasted out there on her own?''

A grinding stab of grief went through Kelly. He drew back his fist and sent it rocketing straight into Baker's jaw. Baker went sprawling, and Kelly stood over him with his aching knuckles cradled in his left palm.

"If you'd done your job, Mohatsa would have been fine," Kelly said low and furiously. "We'd have all been out of here by now. Face it, Baker. You panicked."

Baker squirmed upright and dabbed at the bleeding corner of his mouth. "I'm still alive! That's all I care about—"

"Silence," said the mercenary.

Kelly turned to him at once. "What is it?"

The mercenary's eyes were focused on the distance. He listened intently, then blinked and glanced at Kelly. "Someone coming. Guards, at least two."

Baker got to his feet with a smirk. "They're coming for me. So long, sucker."

Kelly met the mercenary's gaze. "Can we take them?"

The amber eyes gleamed. Without a word, the mercenary took a stance behind the door. Kelly positioned himself on the other side.

"No!" said Baker. "You'll get us all killed if you try anything. 41, we made a deal."

The mercenary shook his head. "You would betray me the first chance you got."

Baker's face turned red. He pointed at Kelly. "Do you think he won't?"

41's gaze sought Kelly's. Kelly wanted his help, but he didn't trust the man. He said nothing to sway the mercenary either way.

"He's got some stupid idea about saving the universe," said Baker contemptuously. "Commander Kelly of Special Operations, Intelligence branch. Son of an admiral. Rich boy playing hero. Earning his fancy medals off the backs of poor dumb grunts who've been sold on a uniform and a legend. The Hawks are a bunch of crap, my friend. You can take that from me—"

"I take nothing from you," said 41 harshly. "Now, be silent."

Kelly heard the guards approach. They were talking to each other in Saluk, laughing and cursing the cold. Pausing outside the door to the shed, they stamped their feet. Kelly tensed, listening to one of them fumble with the lock.

Baker stood in front of the door, glaring at both Kelly and 41. He lifted his fists, but Kelly knew he wouldn't attack either of them. Some of Kelly's contempt must have shown in his face, for Baker caught his eye and reddened.

He drew a sharp breath. "Help!" he shouted. "Help! They're trying to—"

With a growl, the mercenary leapt at Baker in a one-armed tackle and knocked him sprawling. Baker's voice ended in a shrill yelp, then he began to swear loudly as he struggled. Baker fought dirty, crashing his fists into 41's injured arm.

Kelly heard the guards shout something. Holding his breath, he jumped to the other side of the door and pressed himself there, uneasily aware that dealing with the guards was up to him now.

The door flew open, crashing into Kelly. Two troopers ran inside, shouting and swearing. They began kicking at the two men struggling on the ground. Kelly picked his moment and leapt, hitting the back of one trooper and sending him sprawling. The other one whirled with a chilling battle howl and aimed his blaster at Kelly.

Kelly kicked, sending the blaster flying. But the trooper whipped out his dagger and ran at Kelly, who dodged just in time to avoid a slash across his side. He realized the trooper was deliberately aiming low at his belly, where the Salukan heart would have been.

Kelly dodged again, then feinted and darted in close inside the reach of the knife to grapple with the trooper. He got in a good punch to the man's jaw, but it was like iron and Kelly shouted in pain. The trooper slashed at him again. Kelly seized his wrist with both hands and held on, straining to keep that blade from plunging into him.

The other trooper by this time had picked himself up. He grabbed Kelly from behind, holding him for his companion to finish off. Kelly leaned his weight on the trooper behind him and curled up his legs to kick the knifer in the midsection. With a whoosh of breath, the guard staggered back, colliding with 41 who by this time had subdued Baker. 41 grabbed him, spun him around, and wrested the knife from his hand by the simple expedient of bringing down the trooper's forearm across his knee like a stick. The snap of bone was sickeningly loud. The trooper collapsed onto his knees with a scream.

Kelly, meanwhile, struggled to get free, but the remaining trooper jabbed him in the kidney with the snubbed nose of his blaster. Kelly froze, his heart beating too fast.

"Enough!" said the guard, jabbing Kelly again. But his command was for 41, who saw the blaster and stopped short.

On the ground, Baker scrambled to his hands and knees. "I wasn't a part of it," he said loudly. "You saw me fighting them. I tried to stop them from attacking you."

"Baker," began Kelly, but 41 whirled and kicked Baker in the ribs.

With a hoarse gasp Baker fell onto his side.

The guard pulled his blaster from Kelly's back and aimed it at 41. "No move," he said in awkward Glish. "*Vasweemi.* Stand over there."

Slowly, holding his hands away from his sides to show he intended no sudden moves, 41 did as he was told. The blaster pressed once again in the small of Kelly's back.

"Now," said the trooper. "I kill you for being trouble."

8

For a moment there lay only silence, broken by 41's harsh breathing and the thunder of Kelly's heart. The blaster eased fractionally from his spine. Kelly knew that was to keep the energy lash from recoiling over the guard's hand when he fired. Kelly's mouth went dry. He tried to swallow and couldn't.

Baker got to his feet, groaning and clutching his side. He scowled at 41. "You caved in my ribs, you son of a—"

"Enough!" roared the guard. "No speak. You get your chance to die, *vasweemi*, one at a time."

Baker's mouth fell open. He stared a moment, then shook his head. "No," he said. "You don't understand. I'm special. The minlord is going to talk to me."

"We have orders. All prisoners to the mines. Troublemakers die," said the guard. "This one first. Then you. Then—"

"No!" said Baker. "You can't. I tell you I'm not one of them. The minlord wants to know about our ship."

The guard laughed harshly and pointed his blaster at Baker. "The minlord has seen your ship. A pathetic thing, suitable for kuprat-eaters. Your ship is destroyed—"

A roar of protest came out of Kelly. He snaked his right leg back between the guard's and turned, tripping the man off balance. The blaster fired, and Baker fell with a scream. Kelly threw himself on the guard and managed to chop him across the throat. The guard sprawled unconscious, and Kelly picked himself up slowly.

Panting a little, he stared at the downed Salukans, and his

rage faded to numbness. First Caesar, and now Siggerson and Beaulieu. That left himself and maybe Mohatsa. Baker was right; dead squads were getting to be characteristic. Was he losing his judgment and perspective? *Was* he Killer Kelly?

41 crouched beside Baker and touched his throat. ''Baker is dead.''

Kelly stared at Baker, but instead he kept seeing the faces of the old squad and the new.

Rising to his feet, 41 walked over to Kelly. ''This is our chance. Let us go before they are missed. Get their weapons.''

Kelly lifted his gaze to 41's and read impatience there. He knew he had to pull himself together. From the first they had all known the risks. But telling himself that didn't help.

''We could have waited for the *Omu Donde* to get here. But, no, I had to mount an assault.''

''You're a fool,'' said 41. He bent over the guards and took their weapons and a wig which he crammed on his head. ''Quickly. Put on one of their uniforms. Then we can walk out of here.''

Surprised out of his self-pity, Kelly stared at 41. ''I'm too pale to pass as a Salukan.''

''In the storm, who will notice?''

That made sense. Kelly bent and began stripping one of the guards. The uniform was too big for him, but it would go on over his own clothing. In this cold an extra layer was welcome.

''There's no point in trying to steal back the wristbands,'' Kelly said. ''Without a ship to teleport to we're—''

''*Darshon,*'' said 41, crouching to help Kelly as much as he could with one hand. He looked pale himself beneath his bronzed skin. A sheen of thin sweat coated his forehead. ''I counted on your ship. Your crew should have taken more care.''

''Care!'' Kelly pulled on the leggings with swift yanks. ''Siggerson was a damned fine pilot. The fact that he put us into orbit without detection ought to speak for him.''

41 shrugged. ''He didn't stay undetected. That is the last word. Space Hawks are supposed to be the best. In my career I have been careful to avoid people like you. Now I think perhaps I was too careful.''

Kelly shrugged his way into the tunic and struggled with the unfamiliar closures. 41 was trying to provoke him; a lot of idiots liked to play the game of picking a fight with a Hawk just to say they'd done it.

"You aren't stupid," Kelly said, his voice muffled as he bent over. "Drop the game."

"Then pull yourself together," said 41 just as sharply.

Startled, Kelly glanced at him. 41's tawny eyes had narrowed to slits. Despite the wig he looked feral, almost threatening. Unpredictable, Kelly realized with sudden caution. Many mercenaries were either fleet dropouts, psychopaths, or bad products of mixed gene stock who slipped through the cracks of civilization.

"All right," said Kelly slowly. "Step one is to get out of this complex. You mentioned a resistance movement—"

"Yes."

"Good enough. If we can join up with them, we can hold out until the fleet gets here. But unless you've got an idea of direction, we could wander out there in the snowdrifts for a long time."

"I know where to go," said 41, looping the sash over Kelly's head and shoulder. "I told you I escaped the mines with a woman. She meant to go to the resistance group. North, she said." 41 paused and met Kelly's gaze. "We should go north also."

Kelly straightened and held out his hand for one of the blasters. To his relief 41 handed it over. "Fine. Maybe some of them can give me information about Kevalyn—"

41 put his hand on Kelly's arm and stared at him. "Kevalyn?"

"Why, yes," said Kelly quickly. "Do you know her? Have you seen her? Kevalyn Miscetti, about so tall with dark hair and gray eyes?"

"She escaped from the mine with me."

A burst of relief went through Kelly, loosening a knot that had ridden low in his gut since he left Station 4. He laughed. "Good for her! I should have known better than to worry. Kevie's too much like the old man."

The depression that had threatened to settle over him faded. He couldn't balance Kevalyn's life against those of his squad and say one was worth more than the others. But if she survived, that gave him something left to reach for.

41 watched him with that closed, wary expression again. "She is special to you?"

Kelly glanced up. How to explain that Kevie had been his protective big sister, that she had taught him how to sneak out of the house at night, that she had cheered him on at his school soccer games, that she had always taken his side in any argument, that she tutored him in calculus and cried the day he graduated from the Academy? He smiled, thinking of those good times and of others when she'd furiously fought him and won, of when her marriage went sour and she turned up at his place in the rain like something lost.

"Yes," he said. "Very special. If you got her out of the mine, then I owe you a great deal." He held out his hand.

41 drew back with a slight frown and tossed a wig at him. "I see. You ready?"

The wig stank of sweat and some kind of sickly sweet perfume. Grimacing, Kelly put it on then stood between 41 and the door. "I have a policy about mercenaries," he said. "I don't trust them and I keep clear of them as much as possible. But if you help me find her, I'll see you get off Chealda. If you're wanted, I'll try to get that—"

"You have that much influence?" broke in 41 quickly. "What Baker said is true? Your parent is an admiral?"

Kelly flushed. "Yes. I don't use my family connections often. But I do pay my debts. Deal?"

"I am not wanted," said 41 proudly. "But to be stranded on Chealda looking for work is not good. Deal."

Kelly did not try again to shake hands with 41. Instead he nodded and headed for the door with his blaster in his hand. "Then let's go."

Outside, the wind shrieked about them, blinding them with snow and chilling them to the marrow. Gasping for breath, Kelly lifted a hand before his face and tried to see.

Most of the complex was unlit, but the snow reflected even the most minute light into a pale, diffuse glow. The smell of smoke and wet ashes overcame the sharp cleanness of the air. In the distance beyond the barracks a mover roared as it shoved collapsed walls and debris into a pile. Its headlights stabbed through the blurry snowfall as it circled and pushed over another ruined building. Troopers huddled about the orange flames of bonfires that strobed their figures into silhouettes.

"You see?" said 41 into Kelly's ear. "Good destruction work. What kind of artillery did you use? A short cannon?"

Kelly glanced at him and saw a lean profile shadowed against the night. "We need an airsled. We can't walk in this weather."

41 shook his head. "Sleds are for officers. Why not steal a carrier instead?"

"The roads are out," said Kelly. "My team blew them with Klopers."

"You had a good team," said 41. "We would have no problem in taking a carrier, but a sled may get us caught."

"We have nothing to lose," said Kelly grimly.

He started forward, walking with his hand resting lightly on the butt of his blaster. 41 kept pace although he seemed to be limping. He made an effort to hold himself straight and he carried his injured arm down naturally at his side. Kelly approved. This was one tough, smart mercenary. Whether he could be trusted remained to be seen.

Kelly hoped their disguises would get them across the complex unchallenged, but they'd barely gone more than a hundred meters before a trooper carrying a percussion rifle blocked their path. The translator implant beneath Kelly's jaw told him they were being asked for the password. He hesitated, glancing at 41.

The mercenary barked out an obscenity in Saluk. He was loud enough to catch the attention of the troopers huddled by the bonfire.

"You spawn of a barbarian! What password? We have walked all the way from that hole to hell the minlord calls a mine and we are cold and exhausted. Do you greet us as brothers? No, you speak to us as though we are kuprat-eaters and challenge our honor."

The sentry looked confused. He glanced over his shoulder, but no officer was nearby. "I do not understand," he said at last. "The mine? What has happened there?"

41 flung wide his good arm. "What has happened here?"

"The mine attacked? *Darshon!*" The sentry spat in sympathy and lowered his rifle. "We have heard no such news—"

"Comm is out," said 41. "The oparch sent us as messengers. I am wounded, and this man breathed so much radex gas he cannot speak."

Kelly obligingly coughed. He did not have to fake his shivering.

"Come then, brothers," said the sentry in concern. "I shall take you to the cooks. We have no barracks, but—"

41 lifted his hand in a gesture that was pure Salukan. "Keep to your duty. Let us do ours."

The sentry stepped aside, and they went past him. As soon as they were back in the shadows and out of earshot, Kelly leaned toward 41.

"Good acting," he said quietly.

He drew his blaster. 41 threw him a quick look, but made no reply. They walked faster through the whip of snow.

In the lot, two ore carriers stood like silent behemoths. Beyond them, the mover continued to shove debris and wreckage into piles. 41 leaned against the shoulder-high treads, sheltering himself from the wind, and hugged his injured arm. Kelly walked past him and squinted, looking for an airsled. He saw only one, parked beneath an awning that shuddered and flapped in the wind. A sentry stood guard over it. Kelly grinned to himself and pointed.

"How about the minlord's own sled?" he asked.

41 pried himself away from the carrier and joined Kelly. "If we can get it, no one will fire on us. If it carries his crest, it represents his person."

"Then we take it," said Kelly.

In silence 41 gestured at the guard.

"Two against one," said Kelly. "Can't beat the odds."

41 said nothing, and fresh suspicion flared in Kelly. He drew his blaster on 41 and seized him by the shoulder, whirling him around and pressing him against the side of the carrier.

"What's the matter, mercenary?" he asked. "Lost your nerve?"

41 bared his teeth and moved quicker than Kelly expected, numbing Kelly's forearm with a swift blow and dodging free. They faced each other angrily.

"Are you with me or not?" demanded Kelly.

"Why are you so suspicious? Is there truth to what Baker called you?"

Kelly stiffened, but with effort he controlled his temper. An argument here could get them caught at any minute. He was freezing and hungry and tired. He wanted out of here, at any cost.

Stepping around 41, he ran toward the sentry, brandishing his blaster and yelling, *"Hut! Hut! Avi!"*

"Ouesa?" asked the startled sentry, moving toward him.

At the last moment, Kelly gestured behind him and pretended to stumble. The sentry reached out reflexively to catch him, and Kelly dragged him to the ground. He chopped swiftly, but his blow glanced off the sentry's thick wig. Cursing, the sentry seized Kelly by the throat and squeezed. Struggling desperately, Kelly tugged at the sentry's fingers, trying to release that relentless pressure. But the sentry only squeezed harder, cursing him all the while. Kelly gasped, his lungs straining now. The world began to go light then dark, blurring around him. He could hear a loud roaring in his ears. The pain in his chest increased, and there was nothing, not one trick or wrestle hold he could use that worked against his opponent.

Faintly he heard the sound of footsteps crunching over the frozen ground and a deep thud. The sentry grunted and fell beside Kelly, wheezing hoarsely with all the breath knocked out of him. The sudden air in Kelly's lungs almost made him dizzy. Gasping, he struggled to sit up, then nearly fell over in a fit of coughing.

41 jumped over him and struck the sentry again, knocking him unconscious. "Hurry," he growled. He began dragging the sentry through the snow toward the airsled.

Still savoring the sweet ability to breathe again, Kelly massaged his throat and got to his feet. He ran ahead of 41 and ducked under the awning. The airsled had been designed to hold the minlord, his pilot, and at least two bodyguards without sacrificing much of the slim lines necessary for coefficient air drag. It was capped with a plexi-dome, allowing the passengers to ride in complete comfort and climate control. Its sleek sides gleamed faintly.

Kelly slid his hand over the door and felt the intricate,

embossed crest. Letting out his breath, he hit the hatch release. In smooth quiet the hatch lifted, and a faint interior light came on. Kelly slid into the pilot's seat, finding that he had adequate leg room but slightly different contours than the seat had been designed for. The control panel was complex, but he found the gauge that registered power levels. It looked like the airsled ran on solar power. Kelly frowned in dismay. They were sunk.

41 dragged the sentry under the awning and dropped him beside the airsled. He peered in at Kelly and gestured. "Help me fit him into the back. If he's missing with the sled, it will confuse matters and maybe give us more time."

"Forget it," said Kelly. "It's solar."

"You sure?" 41 leaned in over Kelly to look at the controls himself. "No engine back up?"

"Not on a four-seater. Damn," said Kelly bitterly.

"If the cells are big enough, there should be some power storage," said 41.

Kelly sat up straighter. "Enough to get us out of here?"

"Think so."

Kelly met 41's gaze. "Then let's do it."

Five minutes later, with the sentry bound and gagged with their uniform sashes, 41 took the controls and edged the airsled out from beneath its protective awning.

Beside him Kelly kept a sharp lookout and tensed as he saw several troopers look in their direction. "Blast this baby out of here now."

41 gunned the airsled, lifting her up and forward so sharply Kelly feared they would stall. But the airsled screamed up through an alley, clearing the few standing storage tanks by scant meters. Kelly clutched the restraint bar and shut his eyes, but they didn't crash.

The airsled rolled over in a tight arc, and a klieg switched on at ground level in the complex missed them. The powerful light swung their way, but 41 heeled the airsled over in the opposite direction and they dived over a ridgetop low enough for Kelly to imagine their belly scraped gravel. Swooping down the other side, 41 kept the airsled on a hair-raising course parallel to the ridge, dipping and lifting just enough to clear boulders or the stunted skeletons of trees.

Kelly's mouth dried out, but he said nothing. He knew that

41 was keeping low in these gullies to elude tracking scans. But they couldn't do this for long. A gust of snow-laden wind rattled them, nearly pushing them into the side of the ridge, and Kelly flinched. 41 grunted and hung on grimly to the steering bar. They bumped in spite of his efforts, but he regained control almost instantly and gunned the throttle to lift them a couple of meters.

The canyon twisted in the wrong direction and with an oath 41 wrenched the steering bar forward. The airsled shot straight up, leaving Kelly's stomach somewhere in the bottom of the gulch. It rolled and leveled, clearing another ridgetop by a dangerous margin, and jerked as crosswinds buffeted it. Visibility was practically nil between the darkness and the snow. 41 hadn't switched on any running lights. Kelly felt blind as he tried to peer outside, but 41's night vision seemed to be adequate to the job.

''How much reserve?'' asked 41.

His mouth tightened as he steered them in a starboard curve and shot down into another canyon.

''We've used half of what we've got,'' said Kelly. A cluster of blips flashed onto the scanner screen, and Kelly leaned forward. ''Damn! We've got pursuit.''

41 pulled off his wig and tossed it in the back. ''How many?''

''Three. Small register.'' Kelly frowned as he adjusted the scanner. ''Patrol scooters?''

41 grunted.

''Those will be hard to shake off. I make them at a quarter of a mile, and closing.'' Kelly glanced up. ''We don't want to lead them where we're going.''

''We're not going to get *there*,'' said 41. Shaking back his long hair, he leaned closer to the forward windshield and squinted. ''We're running out of power too fast. We'll have to land and wait till daylight to power up again. Do you see any level terrain?''

Kelly's throat nearly locked up. ''No. We studied the topography of this region before we came in. Your best bet is to come down in a valley.''

''We don't have time to hunt for one,'' said 41. Sweat beaded his temples, and his face was drawn with strain.

"They are tracking us by our power curve. If we shut down, they go blind."

"Shut down?" Kelly stared at him. "You can't do a powerless landing in this weather. The wind will tumble us."

41 bared his teeth. "What choice do we have? I'm not going back into the mines to be worked without rest like an animal, to be flogged for their entertainment, to starve for water while I sweat myself into dehydration. How close are they now?"

Kelly looked. "An eighth of a mile."

"We have to do it now, or we'll never shake them." 41's hand slammed the throttle before Kelly could come up with another protest.

The cessation of power stilled all vibration within the airsled, and for a moment Kelly heard nothing but the muffled roar of the wind outside. They dropped in what felt like a controlled dive, then the crosswinds caught them. The airsled twisted viciously in spite of 41's efforts to hold it, but it didn't tumble.

Kelly reached across 41 and touched the controls for the guidance flaps. At once they could feel the drag of resistance, slowing their impetus, and 41 was able to steady them.

But they were dropping fast, and at this trajectory Kelly didn't think they had far to go before they hit ground. They bumped the side of a ridge, scraping metal in an ear-splitting screech, and rolled over.

"*Darshon!*" shouted 41. "Throw your weight!"

Clinging grimly to his restraint bar, Kelly did his best to shift his weight upward. 41's shoulder bumped his as 41 did the same. The airsled responded slightly, then they bellied and any small bit of control remaining was lost.

The airsled slewed wildly and tumbled. Kelly's head banged into the side hard enough to bring him to the edge of blackout. He hung on to consciousness, trying his best to brace himself as they rolled and slithered. The stern bumped over a small boulder with enough impetus to flip it up. For a moment Kelly feared they were going to go end over end. The airsled wasn't built for much crash resistance. At any minute she could crumple or break open.

His restraint bar came loose, and Kelly grabbed wildly at any hold he could find. But he was rattled around inside the cockpit until he was too dazed and disoriented to brace himself. Vaguely he became aware of 41 shouting something, but he couldn't make it out.

Then they seemed to slam into a wall. Everything stopped and grew still, and for Kelly there was nothing at all.

9

Slowly Kelly's battered consciousness grew cognizant of the fact that they'd quit moving. The airsled seemed intact, and he at least was alive. He was wedged nearly upside down with his head crammed behind the front seats at a painful angle.

Not quite certain why he hadn't broken his neck, Kelly began maneuvering himself free. It took awhile, since at that angle he couldn't get enough leverage to pull himself out. Straining until he was breathless and gasping, he finally righted himself and slid down in his seat. His head throbbed with the pressure of too much blood, but that drained back to normal and Kelly wiped his face with unsteady hands.

It was pitch dark in the airsled. From the angle of things they were canted at about forty-five degrees with Kelly on the high end. Outside, the wind howled and clawed at the plexi-dome. The rattle of snow sounded more like sleet now. With the heat shut off, cold seeped inside. Kelly shivered.

"41?" he said.

He got no answer. Frowning, Kelly reached out, groping for the mercenary. His fingers closed on the thick, coarse weave of Salukan cloth and tightened. He had 41 by the arm. He shook it, but 41 did not stir.

Kelly pulled his hands up to his mouth and blew on them. Then he started a systematic search by feel of the interior of the airsled until he found small storage compartments fitted into the sides near the floor. Opening these, Kelly fingered through the contents. At last he found what he was looking for. Snapping on the small hand torch, he blinked in the sudden illumination and dimmed it as much as possible.

It would be pretty stupid to wave lights around for the patrol scooters to find. Cupping his left hand loosely over the end of the torch to dim it even further, Kelly checked the sentry in the back seat. The man's head was twisted at an angle that told Kelly he was no longer a problem.

Kelly shone the light at 41. The mercenary lay slumped over his restraint bar. Gripping his shoulder, Kelly gently tugged him upright. Dark blood seeped from an abrasion on 41's forehead. Kelly patted him gingerly to search for broken bones. As he touched 41's left side, the mercenary stirred but did not awaken. Kelly found his pulse rapid but could not judge whether that was normal.

While he was at it, he searched 41 for identification or snoop devices. He found neither. Frowning, Kelly considered that this was his best chance to ditch 41. But if the mercenary was on the level, then he was too valuable an ally to abandon.

The temperature continued to drop rapidly. Kelly rubbed his arms briskly to keep his circulation going. From the sound of the wind, the storm had not abated. Depending on their position and the rate of snowfall, they could find themselves buried by morning. Kelly hit the hatch release.

It opened reluctantly, grinding a bit against the weight of snow. Kelly pushed it from the inside and the hatch finally lifted. A freezing blast dissipated the last lingering bit of warmth inside the sled. Shivering, Kelly climbed out on legs that were more wobbly than he expected. He staggered and nearly fell. Righting himself, he turned and lowered the hatch but did not secure it.

The snow drifted deep here. He sank up to his knees and floundered a bit with his first few steps until he got the hang of dragging his legs through the snow instead of lifting his feet completely out for each step. His toes went numb almost at once. Grateful for the warmth of his wig, he tucked his hands beneath his arms and plowed a path to about six meters from the craft.

Turning his back to the wind, he squinted in an effort to see. He found the skid marks down the hillside where they had tumbled. Shaking his head at their luck, Kelly climbed to the top of the ridge and crouched there. Chapped with cold, his face felt as though it would crack if he changed expression. His teeth chattered uncontrollably. The wind chill was dangerous. But he didn't intend to freeze to death out here if he could help it.

During a momentary lull, he listened but heard no scooters overhead. It looked as though they had lost them. But at what cost? Kelly glanced over his shoulder and stared at the airsled wedged in the bottom of the canyon.

The urge to huddle up and conserve energy sapped his willpower. That was the wrong thing to do, however.

Straightening, he swung his arms about and did a few jumps. He was about to pick his way back down the slope when he glimpsed something from the corner of his eye. Pausing, Kelly turned and cupped his hands about his eyes to shield them. Over to his right, the ground rose, leveling into a tiny mesa. Probably 41 had tried to land them there before he'd been tumbled into the gully. By straining his eyes, Kelly could just make out a vague shadow of something large there.

Taking careful bearings, he pulled out the hand torch and scrambled toward the mesa. It took awhile to climb to it, but by then he realized he was heading toward a structure of some kind.

The wind dropped speed, and Kelly managed to drag in a few breaths that did not feel as though he'd been knifed in the lungs. He felt sleepy and very tired, but he forced himself to ignore these signs of hypothermia.

Stumbling on frozen feet, he shone the torch on the building. Built of stone, it was massive, alien, and long abandoned. Part of it had fallen in, but what remained had plainly been designed to inspire awe. Kelly tilted back his head to stare up at the vaulted arches and massive columns that appeared to have been hewn from single stones of immense size.

He could only describe it as a temple. He reached out and touched a plinth with his frostbitten fingers. He knew Chealda's native population died out centuries ago; this stood as a testament to their vanished civilization.

At the moment, however, shelter remained a priority. He went cautiously inside, alert for any signs of structural instability or indications that animals had a lair here. But the place seemed truly abandoned. The cold gave it a clean smell. His boots crunched on frozen snow and grit layering the stone floor. Already he felt better out of the wind.

The layout looked simple: a wide, columned hallway down the center, with multiple alcoves leading off each side. Kelly entered one of these and found a small cubed stone vaguely reminiscent of an altar with a drain channel carved into the floor. There were no windows, no other door, no other features. Kelly flashed the torch about and decided it would do as a place to spend the night. Now all he had to do was get 41 here.

Kelly waited a few moments to rest and thaw himself. Blowing on his fingers and wriggling them, he wanted to sit down and never move. The idea of facing that cold outside again daunted him, but 41 would freeze to death in the airsled if Kelly left him there.

With a groan, Kelly pushed himself back onto his feet and started out of the temple. But as he turned into the central hallway, he felt a warm draft coming from somewhere. He frowned and touched his cheek. Hallucinating? No, he felt it again, a faint stir of warm air. Kelly swung around and headed on along the hallway. His torchlight stabbed here and there, picking out a carved face peering down from the ceiling, a frieze detail of abstract designs, a metal bowl lying forgotten on the floor.

The farther he went, the warmer became the air blowing in his face. Kelly quickened his pace and found himself at last in a room about twenty feet square. The warmth in the room enveloped him. He stretched out his arms to soak in as much as possible.

The floor had several levels, broken into steps leading up and down with open holes like vents through which steam rose. Below his feet he could hear a faint burble of water. He crouched to shine the light down through one of the vents. The heat source appeared to be an underground spring of hot water. Stone benches ran along the walls. A purification chamber?

He stayed there as long as he could, then hurried out into the cold to get 41. The storm had ended while he was inside. The hush of the night startled him when he emerged, for around him lay the absolute quiet of nature. The air was heavy with cold, incredibly clean and sharp as he drew breath. It almost burned his nostrils, it was so cold. But his body still radiated the heat from the purification chamber and he hardly felt the low temperature yet. His breath puffed around his face, and he glanced up at the sky, which was clearing to show stars and tiny slivers of the dual moons.

Snowdrifts blanketed the world in eerie white that seemed to glow in the darkness. It was a pale, silent nightscape, breathtakingly beautiful.

Kelly shook himself free of the spell and floundered forward, sinking deep into the snow that rechilled his wet clothes and numbed his feet. Snow had not quite filled his tracks, so he was able to follow them back to the airsled.

By the time he arrived he was so chilled and tired he dropped to his knees in the snow and just leaned against the hatch. All he wanted to do was sleep. Just for a little while.

The hatch opened, knocking Kelly over. The shock of snow down his neck roused him from his drowsiness. He lifted his head and saw 41 holding a blaster on him. Anger stirred beneath his lethargy.

"Great," he mumbled. "I freeze to death to come back so you can shoot me. That's gratitude."

He let his head fall back in the snow and waited, but 41 didn't shoot.

"Get up," said 41. "Get up or I will close the hatch and keep you out. Then you really will freeze."

Kelly's brain woke up enough for alarm signals to go off. This lethargy meant he was dying. He had to get up. Had to do what 41 said.

Slowly he managed to roll over. Even more slowly he got to his hands and knees. He no longer felt cold, and that frightened him.

"41," he said. His lips were so stiff he could barely speak. "Found . . . shelter. Warm there. . . ."

"How far?" said 41, then he muttered something in a language Kelly's translator did not recognize. "You're hallucinating. You're warm because you're dying of cold."

"No." Kelly felt himself sinking down again and resolutely stiffened his elbows to hold himself up. "Hot spring water . . . temple over the . . . ridge."

41 pushed the hatch all the way open and climbed out.

Kelly watched him with relief, glad to know he didn't have to carry the mercenary. Maybe 41 would carry him.

But 41 leaned against the side of the sled and put his hand to his head. "How long have you been gone?" he muttered. "I must have been out longer than I thought."

"Follow my tracks," said Kelly. "The mesa—"

"I tried to land there," said 41, dropping his hand to his side.

"Yeah, I figured that. Did you see the ruins there?"

"No."

"We'll have shelter. One room is warm." Kelly dragged himself upright and reached out. "Come . . . little time."

41 did not move. "There is nothing. You're mad."

"And you're not thinking straight," snapped Kelly. "Why should I lie?"

"I do not know," said 41, looking at him. "Why should you?"

"I don't need this," said Kelly in disgust. He started walking away.

He had nearly reached the top of the ridge before 41 came after him.

"Stop this. You're mad," said 41. His voice sounded raw with weariness. "Is it the way of Space Hawks to walk out to meet death?"

Grabbing the scrawny top of a bush sticking out above the snow, Kelly made it to the top of the ridge and stood there shivering.

He pointed. "There, damn it. Look at it."

41 came to a halt beside him. In the distance, the shadowy outlines of the temple stood in dark contrast to the whiteness of the world.

"Ah," said 41 softly. "A place for the—"

The overhead roar of scooters caused him to break off. Glancing around wildly, Kelly could not see them but they were approaching fast.

"They've picked us up!" he shouted. "Run for it!"

41's arm swung out and blocked him from scrambling down the slope. "Run where? There's no cover out here, and their heat trackers will pick us up anyway."

Kelly shook free and glared at him. "What are you going to do? Sit here and wait for them to take pot shots at you?"

He started down the slope, scooting on his seat and scrambling the rest of the way. At the bottom, he lost his balance and tumbled over and over in the snow, emerging breathlessly only to duck again as the scooters passed directly overhead.

There were two of them, both equipped with searchlights that reflected off the snow with blinding whiteness. Kelly ducked and dodged, lifting himself up to run again. But the snow was too deep, and he floundered. Falling into a drift, he waved with one arm in a frantic effort to get upright. The scooter hovered right above him, shining its light over him. Cursing, expecting to get slagged at any moment, Kelly struggled to draw his blaster.

But before he could get to it, the scooter unaccountably veered away and joined the other, which was circling over 41. A shot rang out, and snow vaporized into steam less than an arm's length from 41. He rolled frantically, but the second scooter headed him off, firing a shot just short of him so that he had to turn back.

It was a cruel game of cat and mouse. As soon as the riders tired of it, they would finish 41 off. But Kelly wondered why they were ignoring him.

His wig, he realized suddenly. He still wore his complete disguise, while 41's blond mane clung in wet strands to his neck. Apparently the riders mistook Kelly for the sentry they'd kidnapped.

Drawing his blaster, Kelly struggled up the slope to where 41 managed to dodge a shot yet again. His movements were slowing, however. He couldn't keep this up much longer.

Puffing, Kelly threw himself to his knees and fired at one rider hovering less than ten feet above the ground. The man fell with a scream, sending his scooter bucking up. It stalled in midair and crashed. Ducking the flying bits of it, Kelly turned on the second scooter. Its rider was already slewing around, gunning the scooter in an attempt to gain altitude. 41 and Kelly fired simultaneously, catching him in the middle. Rider and scooter crashed almost on top of 41, who scrambled frantically out of the way.

Kelly dragged himself to his feet and checked the rider of the nearest scooter. The Salukan lay in a sprawl with his neck at a wrong angle. Kelly glanced at 41, who was limping to the other Salukan.

''Dead?'' Kelly asked. His voice was hoarse from running.

41 nodded and came toward Kelly. His breath fogged about him, and his face was pale with exertion. He looked unsteady on his feet. Involuntarily Kelly reached out for his arm, but 41 slapped his helping hand away and sprang at Kelly's throat.

''Now do you believe me?'' he shouted, giving Kelly a good shaking before Kelly broke free. ''When they try to kill me, does that convince you I am not a Salukan agent? Will you now stop giving me looks of suspicion? I have never worked for them. Always I—''

''The hell you say!'' Furious, Kelly stepped back, clutching his throat. ''You're half Salukan. That's plain for anyone to see. And your story about what you were doing here is thin. You aren't—''

''I am human!''

Kelly frowned. ''Don't take me for a fool. You've got mixed blood, whether you choose to acknowledge it or not.''

''And that automatically makes me one of them.'' 41 sneered. ''You have a little mind, Commander.''

''No, but Salukans don't mix much with other races. If—''

''I was raised by neither side!'' snapped 41. ''I have no loyalty to political factions. Money buys me, nothing else.''

''That's what I'm afraid of.''

41 raised his fists. ''You think these Salukan *kuprats* hired me to spy on you?'' He spat. ''That for what you think.''

''You still haven't told me what you're doing on Chealda.''

''Yes, I—''

Angrily, Kelly gestured to cut him off. ''No, the truth. Supply ships are company owned and protected. They don't hire mercenaries for escort service. There are only two reasons for you to be here. One is that you're a Salukan spy. The other is that you're a pirate.''

41's mouth tightened. He faced Kelly with his head held high, and in his tawny eyes shone a mixture of defiance, resentment, and guilt. In the silence, Kelly aimed his blaster at 41's gut.

''Which is it?'' he asked.

41's cheeks stained a dark bronze. He swallowed convulsively a couple of times as though too angry to speak. ''You make a game of me,'' he said finally, his voice low and furious. "Already you know the answer. Why do you insist on confession? Does it make a bigger man of you?"

"All right," said Kelly. "You're a pirate. Just like the Salukans—"

"No! Not like those *darshon*," said 41. He met Kelly's gaze, then averted his own. "You do not understand," he said.

Kelly's brows drew together. In a quieter voice he said, "Try me."

41 glanced at him sharply. "So after suspicion comes pity. You can go to—"

"Yes, I probably will," broke in Kelly. "But not today."

41 sighed as though pushed past his endurance. "Sometimes there is no work on the fringes. Sometimes a man must do desperate things, dishonest things to survive. I had a captain to work for until last year. Since then. . . ." He frowned and shook his head. "What are a few pounds of ore to Satter Consortium? They mine tons. It does not take much to feed one man. They would not have missed it."

This time Kelly dropped his gaze first, embarrassed at having pushed 41 to such an admission. He masked his discomfiture by holstering his blaster.

"The Salukans," said 41, "came here to plunder, to take everything. Are you one who believes that a little theft is as wrong as a big one?"

Kelly looked up at that. He met 41's gaze. "What do you believe?"

41 made no answer. After a moment, Kelly jerked his head. "Come on," he said. "Let's get to that shelter."

They walked in silence through the snow, shivering together, now and then giving each other a helping hand. When they reached the temple at last, Kelly roused his exhausted body to hurry inside. He was eager to reach that warm room.

But 41 hung back, frowning at the vaulted edifice before them. "This is a place for the Old Ones. It should not be violated."

Kelly snorted. "Sit outside and freeze. I don't think getting warm will violate anything sacred here."

He hurried ahead, stumbling in his fatigue. 41 followed a good distance back, his slow footsteps echoing in counterpoint to Kelly's quicker ones.

The purification chamber hissed with steam, bathing Kelly with warmth he could not at first feel. For a moment he was disconcerted, then he realized that he was dangerously chilled.

Placing his torch on the stone bench so that its light shone across the chamber, Kelly pulled off his wig and fumbled to remove his clothes. Naked and shivering, he crawled out to the center of the stone grid and crouched in the midst of the steam, groaning with pain as his frozen extremities began to thaw. He could only hope he wouldn't lose any fingers or toes.

41 entered the chamber. Kelly watched him study their surroundings. Overhead, the roof arched up to an opening perhaps a meter square. Through the shimmer of escaping steam, Kelly could see the velvet night sky with unfamiliar constellations shining like jewels.

''Well?'' Kelly said. ''Isn't this better than freezing to death?''

41 remained by the door, looking as though he might bolt at any moment.

Kelly rose to his swollen feet and winced. ''You'd better get out of your wet clothes.''

41 walked slowly to the bench and sat down near the torch. Something about the way he slumped there reminded Kelly of his injuries. He hobbled across the grid to 41.

''Would you like some help? How bad is that arm?''

41 had closed his eyes. He grunted in response. After a moment Kelly frowned and undid his tunic. Pulling it carefully open, he picked up the torch in his clumsy fingers and shone it on 41's torso. Taut muscles rippled as 41 sucked in a breath. The blaster burn streaked his left side with angry red marks. Kelly started to peel the cloth off 41's shoulder, but stopped at his sharp intake of breath.

''Cut it off,'' said 41 hoarsely.

Drawing the Salukan dagger, Kelly tested the edge with his thumb and started ripping 41's sleeve as gently as he could. By the time he had it slit from shoulder to wrist, both he and 41 were sweating. But 41 did not make a sound.

The blaster burn on his arm had blistered with ugly yellow pus. Infection made the flesh look puffy. Kelly examined it in dismay. He knew rudimentary first aid, of course, but this required serious attention. He was amazed that 41 had managed to function at all, much less occasionally use the arm.

"This is bad," he said. "You need a medic."

41 opened his tawny eyes at that and grunted derisively. "So call the nearest space station."

Kelly tugged his mouth into a smile, but he thought of Beaulieu, lost along with the *Valiant*, and his smile faded quickly. "I wish I could," he said softly.

41 began to shake, and Kelly quickly stripped him of the rest of his clothing. He found a quantity of half-healed cuts across 41's back. One of 41's ankles had been nicked and chafed raw. It now looked almost as ugly as his arm. His bronzed flesh was as cold as stone.

Kelly pulled him upright and put his shoulder beneath 41's good arm. "Let's get you closer to the steam. Maybe it will do something toward cleansing these cuts. Have you got fever?"

41 allowed himself to be supported out onto the grid and lowered to a sitting position where pillars of gentle steam could puff around him. He looked drawn with pain and exhaustion, but his eyes could still flash defiance.

"Condemnation, confession, compassion and mercy," he muttered. "Do you consider yourself a god?"

Kelly drew back from him with an angry frown. "No," he said shortly. "If you don't want my help, just say so."

"So," said 41.

Flushing, Kelly held back a retort and turned away.

"You distrust me," said 41. "Why do you keep saving my life?"

"I told you," said Kelly. "I owe you for helping Kevalyn."

41's expression became one that Kelly could not read. "She is only a woman," he said. "Is she worth so much?"

"Kellys pay their debts of honor. Is that a foreign concept to your culture?"

"What culture?" said 41 bitterly. He looked up at Kelly. "I was orphaned young and raised by nonhumans. I do not know on what planet, only that it was vast grassland steppes where we lived, and very primitive. Later, I was sold into slavery. Then I escaped that and became a mercenary. I have no wealth, no education. What can I be in the life you know?"

Kelly stared at him, unsure of what to answer. It was a bleak upbringing 41 encapsulated in those few words. And in 41's voice he heard a terrible longing that made him realize how advantaged his own youth had been. The finest education and military training, a comfortable home that entertained important and influential people, ambitious siblings, successful parents.

Finally Kelly said, "You can be what you are. There might even be a place for you in Special Operations if you wanted it."

41 snorted. "No."

Kelly raised his brows. "All right. End of conversation."

He moved a short distance away and lowered himself onto the grid, stretching out slowly. His body felt like lead. Already his eyes were closing despite his efforts to stay awake. He sank into a deep, warm blackness.

It seemed like scant seconds later, however, that he was awakened by a kick in the ribs.

"Get up, *vasweem*!" shouted a gruff voice.

He was kicked again.

Disoriented, Kelly sat up and fought his way awake. Already, though, he realized what had happened. Dry-mouthed, he crouched there naked with Salukan troopers ringed about him. Overhead, the green, cloud-streaked sky told him he had slept for hours. He rubbed his gummy eyes, trying to hold down a rising sense of desperation.

"Get up!"

Hastily Kelly complied in time to avoid another kick. Stiffness knotted his body so much he could barely straighten. The troopers laughed at him, jeering and pointing. Kelly refused to be embarrassed by such juvenile mockery. His gaze shifted carefully toward the wall where he had left his clothes and weapons on the bench.

His clothes lay on the floor, and the weapons were gone.

"You can't escape, kuprat-eater," sneered the oparch in his officer's cloak. Cloying perfume oiling his skin filled the air. "You have many trickeries in you, but now you will find them of no avail."

Some of the troopers were shaking 41 awake. He was dragged to his feet. Kelly frowned at him in concern. The yellow pallor to his skin was more pronounced. His eyes shone brightly with fever.

Kelly returned his attention to the oparch. "If you're going to play games with us, forget it. Just kill us and get it over with."

The oparch opened his eyes very wide. Then he smiled, and even his teeth were painted. "Kill you? No, Space Hawk. Instead we will clip your wings. We are taking you to our mind sieve."

Fear flashed through Kelly. To hide it, he lifted his chin and glared at the oparch. "You'll learn nothing."

"Oh, but we will." The oparch smiled wider. "The minlord has ordered you to give us all your knowledge of the Alliance. The sieve will make it so. There is no resisting it . . . unless you want your mind in pieces when you come out."

Kelly made an involuntary move, and two troopers flanked him at once. His arms were dragged behind him and fusion-lock shackles clamped on his wrists.

"Wait!" he said desperately. "You can't take us outside like this. Our clothes—"

The oparch laughed. "If you had wanted your clothes, you should not have removed them. *Uste!*"

The troopers hustled Kelly and 41 forward. As soon as they left the steam chamber, the frigid air seared through Kelly. He began to shake. The stone floor froze his bare feet. Gritting his teeth, he endured it in determination not to beg again.

We should have posted a watch, taken turns, he thought. But even so, he knew neither of them had been in any shape last night to do so.

Kelly glanced over his shoulder at the oparch. "I don't understand," he said. "Why have you gone to all this trouble to recapture us? For all you knew, we could have frozen to death last night and saved you the bother of looking for us."

"But you did not die," said the oparch. He gestured, and the troopers stopped.

Clothing was flung at Kelly. With relief he struggled to pull on the leggings and boots, finding it a difficult task with his arms bound behind his back. The tunic was impossible, but a trooper flung a cloak over him and another over 41.

Another game, thought Kelly angrily. The Salukans loved to make their prisoners twist in as many ways as possible.

"Still," persisted Kelly. "So what if we escaped? We can't warn anyone offworld of your presence. We haven't got a ship now. What harm are we to you?"

The oparch's amusement abruptly faded. He glared at Kelly. "Much harm and much trouble," he snapped. "You and your ship. The minlord will have your mind gutted until you bleed from the ears, Space Hawk. Take them out!"

The troopers shoved Kelly forward, and he stumbled outside where a ground/space shuttle waited with blackened snow melting beneath its exhaust ports. He frowned as he walked, trying to make sense of what lay behind the oparch's anger. What had happened? Something to do with the *Valiant*. Had she survived after all? Had Siggerson fought back somehow? But the little vessel couldn't begin to match herself against a battlecruiser. No, he was deceiving himself with false hope. It was general information the Salukans wanted. And Kelly knew he hadn't a prayer of keeping them from finding out anything they went after.

10

A faint clinking awakened Caesar. Disoriented, he drifted back and forth across the line of consciousness. He was warm and comfortable; he didn't want to wake up.

"Damn it, Horter! Look out!"

The sound of a crash startled Caesar. His eyes flew open, and at the same time he became aware that he was lying half-smothered in snow. He tried to move and found he could not. That scared him spitless. For a minute he thought he was tied up, but he could see his left hand lying next to his face and it didn't have a fusion shackle on it.

Memory seeped back to him, and he frowned in an effort to figure out how long he'd been lying out here in the snow. Long enough to freeze stiff as a board.

Meanwhile, the men making the noise above him on the hill went on with a low-voiced argument interspersed with oaths and muffled yelps of pain.

"I'm telling you, Rolland, if you turn it that way, you'll bugger the screws of that anchor bolt. Easy. *Easy!* Damn, the wind's shifting again. I'll be sick if I have to keep breathing this muck."

"Shut up," muttered Rolland. "Just hold the damned thing steady, and we'll be done quicker."

"You realize," Horter went on, "that the charge on this grav-flat is almost exhausted. It'll bust me up inside if I try to lift this cannon without it. How're we gonna carry it home?"

"Don't worry about it. Damn! Hold it steady, will you?"

"I am," said Horter, aggrieved. "You're turning the release too far. That's why it keeps slipping. I'm gonna be sick. I can't take that smell.''

''Shut up. Just shut up.''

''They've been blown to little bits. Who'd think they'd smell like that in this cold?''

There came the sound of someone being sick. ''Damn you, Horter. You just had to keep talking about it, didn't you?''

''Okay. Okay. I never thought you were so squeamish. Put snow in your mouth. That will help.''

Caesar realized fuzzily that they were speaking Glish, not Salukan. He also figured out that they were stealing his short cannon.

''Hey!'' he said weakly in protest. No one seemed to hear him, so he moved his head a bit and put more lungpower into his voice. *''Hey!''*

The arguing stopped abruptly. Caesar closed his eyes for a second of rest, but when he opened them again he saw a man's knee just inches from his face. A hand held his wrist, presumably checking for his pulse. Caesar blinked, and the man scrambled back.

''Holy mother of— Rolland! He's alive.''

''Can't be. He's frozen stiff.''

''Then why's he blinking at me?''

Feet crunched and squeaked on the snow, then a second man knelt beside him. Caesar tried to move his head so that he could see their faces, but the effort was beyond him. His thoughts faded, but with difficulty he held himself together.

''My . . . cannon,'' he managed to gasp.

''What'd he say?''

''He said it's his cannon. I guess he was the one doing all the shelling.''

''Well, it ain't his cannon now,'' said the voice belonging to Rolland. ''We need it.''

''What kind of uniform is this? Hey, you. Has the fleet come?''

''Never mind that,'' said Rolland impatiently. ''What we need to know is how to release that anchor bolt. It's frozen or something.''

''Geekers, Rolland,'' said Horter. ''Why don't you have the guy walk up there and show you how? He don't even have a pulse.''

Caesar frowned at that information. Was he dead? Was he hallucinating? Every time his thoughts seemed about to sharpen, the world slipped sideways again. But surely he shouldn't be lying out here in this snow. He ought to feel cold and wet. He didn't feel anything.

"Have cannon," he mumbled, "if take me . . . warm."

"He wants us to thaw him out. What about it?"

"We can't carry both him and the cannon back to camp," said Rolland. "You're worried about getting a hernia, remember?"

"Don't be a sap. He blew those Salukans to bits and leveled most of the complex—"

"—yeah, and my core sample equipment with it."

Caesar tried one last time. "Grav-flat . . . set to conserve charge. Take . . . take switch to full. Still enough . . . juice."

"Great!" said Horter excitedly. "How do we release the bolt?"

A queer roaring engulfed Caesar. He tried to hold it back, aware that if he didn't relay the information their deal would be off. He didn't want to die out here on this ice cube. There was a black-furred Shebite waiting for him to come by on his next leave. She kept the best stock of Terran whiskey he'd ever sampled, not to mention her other attractions. For her sake, he struggled to speak, but the roar swept over him and he was gone.

He came to inside a tank of liquid, strapped in and submerged up to his chin. He was screaming, and tears of pain ran down his face. Choking, he struggled a little and managed to stop the noise.

A woman in an unfastened parka stood beside the tank. She watched a hand scanner intently, but when he fell silent she looked up.

"You're awake. Good. Do you want something for the pain? It's better if you don't just yet. We're still waiting for your heart rate to regulate."

He did feel breathless and dizzy. He wanted a painkiller, but she was looking at him with beautiful gray eyes. Somehow he managed to keep himself from begging.

"I'm fine," he choked out, then wriggled as an agonizing

burst of sensation went up his arms. Pins and needles were nothing compared to this.

To distract himself, he glanced around as far as the strap supporting his chin would allow. The room was small and irregularly shaped. Its walls had been hewn from natural stone. Frowning at the chisel marks, Caesar decided he must be in a cave.

"You're Special Operations," she said, glancing again at her scanner and nodding to herself. "The uniform . . ."

"Yeah. Operative Henry Samms of Peregrine Squad Alpha—"

"Caesar!" she said excitedly, tossing down her scanner and coming closer. "You're Caesar Samms. I've heard such tales about you from Bryan."

Caesar stared at her, momentarily forgetting his torture. Of course . . . now that he looked closely he could see the family resemblance. She had the same black hair, the same chin, the same mouth that could set itself with the determination of a mule. Whatever a mule was.

"Kelly's sister," he said softly.

Her slim brows swept up. "Yes, I'm Kevalyn Miscetti. But if you're here, then Bryan must be too. A rescue mission? Was that what all of yesterday's shelling was about? You don't know how welcome you are! What's his frequency band? We'll contact him and let him know you're alive."

"Yo ho," said Caesar. "Those devils took my comm. But do you have a scrambler?"

"No."

"Then it's not a good idea to be sending out signals for the wig-heads to pick up."

She frowned delicately at his term, and he glared back defiantly.

"So I'm a bigot. So what?"

That made her laugh. With her eyes alive with mirth and some color in her face, she lost that scrubbed scientist's look and became beautiful. He caught his breath in admiration and imagined her in a gown cut low and tight. But imagining was all he'd ever do; Kelly would just about make cat meat of him if he tried a pass at her.

"I haven't any love for the Salukans, believe me, Mr. Samms."

"Caesar, please."

She smiled. "All right. Caesar it is. How did you get such a nickname anyway?"

His face flamed hot, and he squirmed in embarrassment. There was no way he was going to tell her, and he hadn't blushed in thirty years.

He started to say something to get her off the subject, but before he could do so a paunchy man in a parka and waterproof boots came running into the room with a slam of the door.

Kevalyn jumped and turned on him. "God, Rege! Can't you slow down to knock once in a while?"

"I'm sorry," said Rege, sounding not sorry at all. He turned analytical blue eyes on Caesar, who shivered and decided ice chips would be more friendly. "So he's finally awake. How's he coming along?"

"Yeah, I'm awake," said Caesar, taking a dislike to him. "Some brandy would warm me up quicker than this fish bowl."

Kevalyn laughed, but Rege snapped his fingers with an irritated expression.

"He sounds recovered to me. We need him out of here as soon as possible."

"Now wait a minute, Rege," began Kevalyn hotly. "There are a few complications—"

"You're no doctor. Don't start creating a big case out of a simple condition of frostbite."

"Frostbite!" She threw up her arms. "The man was frozen. I'm still fascinated that he's alive at all. He shouldn't be. He should—"

"Interesting," said Rege without even looking at her. He was busy staring at Caesar. "You can write him up in a paper on your next vacation. I doubt you'll be able to present it, since cryogenic freaks do occur now and then—"

"I'll show you who's a cryogenic freak!" said Caesar, struggling against his straps. "Let me out of here."

A sudden bout of breathlessness caught him, and he subsided, struggling for air.

Kevalyn reached for her scanner and pushed Rege out of the way. "Look what you've done. I was just getting him regulated. He needs rest."

"We all need rest," snapped Rege, gazing at Caesar without compassion. "Shoot him up with a stimulant and get him on his feet. We're going to be setting up the cannon as soon as we get our attack line into position, and we need him to direct—"

"No," said Kevalyn, staring at him as though he had lost his mind. "Do you realize what you're saying? Even if it were advisable from his health's standpoint, I'm not qualified."

Rege snorted. "Don't quibble."

"Quibble! You just said so yourself."

"Kevalyn—"

"No. He's not going back outside. And you're crazy, all of you, to try an assault on the Salukans."

"Why? This is the perfect chance, while they're still reeling from yesterday's attack. We can finish them off."

"And what about retaliations at Kuupke and Long Sally? Have you forgotten about Talla Mine already?" she retorted. "When they closed it they slaughtered every man, woman, and child at work inside it."

Rege's pale eyes grew even stonier. "I haven't forgotten. We aren't going to sit like sheep and let it happen again."

"You haven't enough weapons. None of you are properly trained—"

"That's where he comes in," said Rege, jerking his thumb at Caesar.

"Fat chance, pal," said Caesar. "I'm not risking my life with a bunch of yo-head scientists trying to play soldier."

"You see?" said Kevalyn.

Rege scowled. "We're taking Caru, and that's the end of it. They've gotten away with enough."

Startled, Caesar looked from one angry face to the other. "Wait just a minute. Caru? The complex we shelled?"

"Yes."

"You're nuts," said Caesar. "Kelly could still be in there."

"What?" squeaked Kevalyn. "How? Why?"

Rege shouldered her aside to glare at Caesar. "You don't know anything of the kind."

"The last time I talked to my commander, he and another operative were inside the complex. I don't budge without his direct orders. And you aren't firing on the place until we've determined that they're clear."

"You have no jurisdiction here," snapped Rege. "Mercenaries, special forces, whatever you call yourself—"

"How about covert cowboys?" suggested Caesar with sarcasm.

Rege flushed scarlet. "You—"

"I mean what I said," said Caesar. "You're amateurs. If you make an assault on their headquarters, you'd better be prepared for some bloody hard fighting."

"With the short cannon—"

"It has one load left in the magazine," said Caesar. "After that, what do you have in mind?"

Rege opened his mouth, then closed it again.

"Yusus," said Caesar scornfully. "That's what I thought. If you get into close-range fighting, those troopers will carve your butt for breakfast."

"That's why we need you," said Rege more quietly. He stared at Caesar. "We need all of your force. How many—"

"What is this? Recruit an army day? Hawks don't come in squadrons. Standard deployment is one squad for scouting and emergency assistance purposes. We're just to hold things until the *Wellington* gets here."

Rege stared at him. "What!"

"Oh," said Kevalyn. The animation faded from her face, and she turned away to stare blindly at her scanner. "I thought the fleet had come."

"Sorry, babe," said Caesar. "This whole thing caught the fleet with their pants down. We just came out here because Satter kept hollering. You've got about four more days to wait. My advice is to hole up."

Rege turned scarlet. "Your advice," he said bitterly. "My fourteen-year-old daughter is in Long Sally Mine. That is, if they haven't killed her by now. Those—" He choked and put his hands to his face.

Kevalyn put her arm about his shoulders. "Don't torture yourself, Rege. She's a strong, intelligent girl. She'll—"

He twisted free. "You got away, so she can? I don't need to listen to drivel like that. We need action, and we need it now." He glared at Caesar, who was frowning. "What about it? You say we're amateurs. That's true, but we're asking for your help."

"We'll help," said Caesar. "But you need all of us. If I can contact Kelly—"

"He could be anywhere," said Rege in protest. "And our comm signals will bring the Salukans right here to us. I can't take that risk."

Caesar sighed. He already knew that much. He also knew his duty lay in helping the miners in any way he could in the absence of fresh orders from Kelly.

"But that doesn't mean I have to put up with guff from a bunch of squats," he said. "I'm the pro. I give the orders."

Kevalyn shook her head. "Caesar, you aren't—"

Caesar ignored her, keeping his gaze locked on Rege. "That's the deal. Take it or leave it."

"I have to take it."

Caesar nodded. "Get me out of this fishbowl and let's go to work. I'll need an inventory of your supplies. Weapons, explosives, that sort of thing."

Rege gestured dismissively. "That's already been dealt with. We're ready to go right now. All we have to do is get you out there. Then as soon as the sortie comes back—"

"Wait," said Caesar. "What sortie? Where? What are they doing?"

"We captured some Salukans yesterday and borrowed their uniforms. Rolland and MacKey have gone into Caru to reset the defense satellite system. If they make it, the system will automatically clear the freighter and their cruiser from orbit. Then I think you'll find the troopers aren't such good fighters." Rege smiled, his eyes alight with zeal. "They'll have no way to get home."

Caesar stared at him. For a moment he was too astonished to speak, then he began to struggle furiously to get out of the tank. Liquid slopped over the sides.

Kevalyn ran to him. "Caesar, stop it! Caesar, what's wrong?"

Caesar lunged, wanting to get his hands on that damned yo-head's throat. "I'll tell you what's wrong," he panted. "Of all the stupid—"

Rege's head snapped up. "Why? We've let them get away with too much. It's time we fought back."

"But not when our ship is sitting up there in range orbit like a sweet little third target to be picked off!" shouted Caesar. Kevalyn looked shocked, and he glared at her. "Get these straps off me."

In silence she began to do so. Rege stood there, and for the first time he looked as though he saw Caesar as a fellow human being. He opened his mouth, then closed it without speaking.

Kevalyn freed Caesar's arms and the central harness that crisscrossed his torso. He glanced down at himself in revulsion. His body had the pale wrinkled appearance of flesh that's been in water too long. He moved to the side of the tank and reached to pull himself out. The resulting agony in his arms and shoulders nearly made him scream.

"You shouldn't—," began Kevalyn, then cut herself off.

As soon as he caught his breath again, Caesar said, "Who's got a comm?"

"Avirlei keeps it," she said. "All our equipment is stored together in the central cavern. It's not far from here."

"Right." Caesar nodded. "I need some clothes."

She brought him his uniform and a parka, then retreated while Rege helped him from the tank. By the time he finished dressing, he was winded and dizzy. Agony shot through his feet and legs with every step; his knees wobbled weakly. Rege shoved him toward a crate, and Caesar sank down on it gratefully.

"Could Avirlei bring the comm set here?" he asked Kevalyn.

"I'll see—"

"No," said Rege. "You can't use it here. If the Salukans trace the signal, they'll wipe out our camp."

Caesar's temper got away from him. "And what about our ship up there, you cold-blooded—"

"I don't have to take your abuse! You military types always think you can swagger in and give everyone orders. Your ship will . . ." Rege's eyes flickered. ". . . will just have to take its chances."

"That's bilge and you know it." Caesar pushed himself shakily to his feet and started for the door. Kevalyn hurried after him, and he glanced at her. "Your brother is either still on Chealda, or he's aboard the *Valiant*. Do you want him to just take his chances?"

Her face crumpled. "That's not fair. Dr. Miramon is just trying to keep all of us alive. And I want to help you."

"Then get everyone ready to evacuate," said Caesar. "How many are living here? Can you assemble them quickly? Have you an alternative place to hide?"

She looked worried and doubtful, but she nodded without subjecting him to a barrage of protests. "I think I can muster us into order. There aren't many."

"The men are ready to fight, not carry out supplies," snapped Rege from behind them.

Caesar swung around and punched him in the stomach. It was a weak blow, perhaps a quarter of his best, but it served to double Rege. Gasping, he staggered a little to one side, and Caesar glared at him.

"Fight?" He hooted. "I'd like to see you ready to fight. Now you see about helping Kevalyn get people organized. As soon as the *Valiant* has her warning, I'll give you all the help you want in blowing the Salukans to bits. But not before. You follow?"

Not waiting for Rege to answer, Caesar walked out of the room. He found himself in a round tunnel that had been made with a machine borer. Lights overhead glowed dimly. He supposed the place had been originally intended for storage.

"To your left," said Kevalyn. She started off in the opposite direction. "Don't branch off, and you'll get there in three minutes."

It took him nearer to twenty, shuffling along on his aching feet. *Be grateful they weren't taken off,* he told himself and emerged from the tunnel into a natural cavern almost big enough to hold half of Caru. It was well lit and dry. Near the center stood a pair of crude tables parallel to each other. Rifles, tool kits, heaters, dirty plates, and a sleeping baby cluttered the tops of them. Glancing around, Caesar noticed perhaps fifteen men clustered here and there. Most of them were human although he noticed two Boxcans towering above the others. They wore parkas with snow goggles slung around their necks and had rifles over their shoulders. They looked impatient.

Caesar, however, had a cold feeling of foreboding in the pit of his stomach. If he called too late . . .

A couple of men glanced his way, but no one immediately moved forward. Caesar filled his lungs.

"Avirlei!" he shouted, and his voice echoed and re-echoed through the cavern.

Activity stopped everywhere as people stared at him, and an Othian came skimming toward him.

Transparent so that his organs and circulatory system pulsed visibly like something out of an anatomy lesson, the Othian wore a gravity box to protect him from the effects of Chealda's density. Inside it, his boneless limbs fluttered in agitation.

"Quiet, idiot you," he said, his voice echoing from his speech synthesizer. "Set up vibrations and bring all stalactites down. No shouting."

"I want Avirlei," said Caesar. "Failing him, I want the comm set."

The Othian slowed down, then paused. His gravity box floated gently up and down. "Avirlei is this one who speaks. The comm is upon the table. But call you cannot—"

"Watch me."

Caesar started past him, but Avirlei blocked his path. "I have said truth. You cannot—"

"I know the dangers," said Caesar, feeling as though time was getting away from him. "It's priority. Now move."

Something in his tone seemed to daunt Avirlei, for the Othian floated aside. Caesar shuffled past, sweating and cursing the slow and agonizing return of full circulation. He shoved aside some of the clutter surrounding the comm. It was a battered old field unit, packed into a sling that enabled it to be carried. Caesar unbuckled this impatiently, then set about putting in the frequency he wanted.

When he hit it, he swallowed and said, "Samms to *Valiant*. Come in, ship. Samms to *Valiant*."

He shouldn't be using names on an open channel, but his growing sense of urgency made him too impatient to try anything more cryptic.

Static answered him, nothing else. He froze in panic, certain he was too late. Then reason reasserted itself, and he carefully checked everything to make sure it was functioning properly. His palms were suddenly wet. Surreptitiously he wiped them on his thighs and tried again.

"Samms to ship. Siggerson, do you read me? Respond please. Anyone, respond."

Nothing.

Avirlei floated closer. "Something is wrong?"

Caesar looked at him blindly. He felt colder now than when he'd been out in the snow. His legs gave way beneath him and he sank onto the rickety bench beside the table.

"I get nothing," he said in a hollow voice. He couldn't think yet. He couldn't take it in. "I'm too late. The defense zone got them. Damn! Of all the stupid, useless things—"

"What?" said Avirlei, staring at him. "What defense zone? Thirty-eight minutes until activation. And our team has risk to not get inside."

It took a moment for that to register. Caesar blinked and frowned at Avirlei. "Say that again."

"Position is not yet achieved. If your ship does not respond, she must be target for Salukan cruiser. Or she has left. And danger which you have put into us is for an unnecessary call."

A Boxcan strode up to them and aimed his sidearm at Caesar.

"Explain this action, please," said Avirlei.

"Yeah," said Caesar without glancing his way. "The ship wouldn't just leave. Not unless . . ."

Had Kelly and the others mopped up and gone back aboard, thinking him dead? If so, they would have moved out of range to wait for the *Wellington*.

By this time a human had joined them. He cleared his throat. "There was a space battle of a sort last night. We could see the flashes in spite of the snowstorm. Probably a couple of torpedoes went into the atmosphere. Didn't last long."

That, then, told another story. Caesar stared at his hands. They were square and freckled, with the nails bitten to the quick. He clenched them, wanting to strike out in grief and frustration. With her waver field, the *Valiant* could not be spotted in orbit. Which meant Baker had betrayed her to the Salukans before Kelly could stop him. Caesar hoped that Kelly had rimmed out Baker's guts. He wished he could do it himself.

What now?

He didn't know. He felt lost. This new squad wasn't even made up of pals like before. He barely knew any of them. But that didn't seem to make much difference to how he felt.

Sitting here in a depression wasn't going to help, however. Caesar rubbed his face fiercely, letting anger and hatred swell inside him.

When he looked up, several men, including Avirlei and Rege Miramon, were staring at him. They blurred, and he had to blink hard to bring them back into focus.

"All right," he said thickly. "What are you looking at? You got any explosives? I'll show you a few things about taking wig-heads apart."

11

The *Valiant* dropped out of distort less than one thousand kilometers from an asteroid belt not marked on the charts. With the collision alarm blaring in his ears, Siggerson cursed and overrode the automateds to regain manual pilot. A glance at the sensors told him the cruiser still clung to his tail.

"Fastest ship in the fleet," he muttered aloud and turned off the klaxon. The Minzanese shipwrights had better start looking at Salukan specs and upgrade the fleet.

The cruiser's heat shift warned him that she was still running armed. By now she would be locking on. Fear choked him, making him sweat. Desperately he shook off the fatigue blurring his mind. There wasn't time to calculate another course. His only chance lay in going straight through the belt.

His mouth went dry. All his career he'd despised the wild-belt jockeys who got their thrills by tangling with asteroids. Sooner or later a pilot that reckless ended up smeared across a couple of parsecs with his ship accrued to the surface of a magnetic rock. Now, however, he opened the engines to maximum sublight speed and plunged in.

It was the worst kind of seat-of-the-pants piloting, and at the same time the most exhilarating. The *Valiant* screamed through a collision course, dodging and rolling at a velocity that allowed him no time for hesitation. The computer assist struggled to keep up with trajectory balance, but warning lights kept flashing all over his master panel. Internal gravity cut out, then came back on. Strapped in according to regulations, Siggerson impatiently cut it off.

It was a large asteroid belt, and he took the central route

in the longest direction, knowing the cruiser would sniff around the fringes while she waited for him to come out. The asteroids were denser now; the ship buffered past some of the spinning rocks with perhaps as few as fifty meters to spare. Over the hum of instrumentation came a steady rattle as dust particles bombarded the hull. The *Valiant* had her first scars now.

Grimly he steered around a moon-sized rock and dropped one hundred meters on the *z* axis, immediately executing a quarter roll to squeeze through two asteroids. They were spinning toward each other, and he fancied as he scooted between them that he felt them nudge the *Valiant*. His heart stopped, and his hands seemed frozen to the controls. One miscalculation and they would crush him. But then he was through, and elation surged up in his throat. He could do this!

In the next second, however, he snatched at his concentration and skidded through a slalom path of rubble. Another warning sounded; something had pierced the outer hull. Automatic patching commenced, but Siggerson kept an anxious eye on any signs of pressure loss.

Ahead, the asteroids thinned and he could see clear space. His sensors were blurred as long as he stayed in the belt; by the same token, the cruiser couldn't spot him either until he emerged. So in effect he was running blind as to her position. She could be sitting right out there ahead of him like a cat at the mousehole. But he had to take the gamble.

Without slackening speed, he rolled past the last obstacle and burst free. Banking sharply enough to make his stomach lurch, he cut speed to dead stop with such an abrupt slack of g-force he nearly blacked out. Clinging desperately to consciousness, he activated the waver shield and sat tensely to see if his plan had worked.

The *Valiant* started to drift back toward the asteroids. Siggerson switched on the automateds to hold her in place. He watched the sensors, blinking rapidly in an effort to keep the readouts in focus. He was so very tired. At some time during the long chase he had lost count of the hours.

The cruiser came into range. Her A shape, so sleek and graceful in time distort, so clumsy in sublight, dwarfed the *Valiant*. She prowled the perimeter, her sensors probing. Siggerson held his breath. Had the Salukans developed sensors that could reach through the cloaking effect of the waver shield?

The sensors pinged them all right. Siggerson jumped. But the waver shield distorted the feedback of the sensors and they reported nothing back to the cruiser. She moved on.

Siggerson's energy faded. He slumped in his seat and closed his eyes, letting his adrenaline shake down. He knew the captain of the cruiser would not give up the hunt for a long time. With orders to let no word of what was happening on Chealda leak out, the captain would be determined to get the *Valiant* at whatever cost. But he hadn't caught her, and he wouldn't now.

Siggerson smiled tiredly to himself. He could sit here for a day or two, then slip a cautious way back to Station 4. Or he could head off to the farthest reaches of Alliance territory, berth the *Valiant* at a shipyard on an independent planet and have her name and registration numbers stripped off. She would be his, prize booty, a hot little ship like he'd always wanted. For the first time in his life he would have the freedom he craved. He could freelance, gathering scientific information for hire, able to come and go as he pleased.

A noise awakened him. He jerked upright in his seat and rubbed his face groggily. According to the chron, four hours had elapsed. He yawned, unstrapped himself, and stood up to stretch. Automated had dimmed the lights on the quarterdeck. He brushed the control, and the lights came back up. Yawning again, he made several quick checks and found everything in order. Sensors did not register the cruiser at all.

Pleased, he climbed down to the lower deck and entered the galley. The designers had evidently intended it as a sort of mess/lounge, for it was more spacious than it might have been. Fitted in a rectangle, one wall curved slightly to follow the hull. A pleasant blue color scheme made the place soothing, and it was fitted with a table large enough to hold the entire squad at once with ample storage and three processors.

Packets lay scattered on the table and floor. Two of them looked as though they had been chewed open. The contents had spilled out in a thawing mess on the floor.

Frowning, Siggerson bent and picked up the packets with

a fastidious grimace. As he straightened he heard the noise again, something faint and not quite definable. The hairs on the back of his neck lifted. He listened, but heard nothing more. Silence pressed in upon him. For the first time, he grew conscious of his own solitude. He thought of spending the rest of his life alone on this ship.

Something ran along the corridor outside. Tossing down the ruined food packets, Siggerson sprang to the door and looked out.

He saw nothing. But something was on board with him. It most certainly had to be an animal of some kind, probably a pet that Baker or Samms had brought with them. Siggerson frowned. No wonder they hadn't wanted to search the ship for a stowaway.

Animals were unsanitary, against regulations, and a nuisance. He wasn't going to share food with this one, whatever it was. If he could catch it, he'd jettison it.

Stepping out of the small galley, he closed the door firmly and retreated down the corridor to a vantage point where he could watch without being immediately visible himself. He settled down to wait. If the creature was still hungry, it would come back.

After twenty minutes, his patience wore thin. He was hungry and thirsty, and he needed more sleep. "Come *on*," he muttered under his breath.

The creature did not return. Waiting another twenty minutes, Siggerson frowned and gave up. He'd have to devise a different trap. Right now, however, he wanted coffee and food.

Returning to the galley, he finished cleaning up the mess. He selected his dinner and put it in the processor. Two minutes later he sat down to eat a steaming platter of rice, vegetables, and pavli cakes.

A soft chittering sound startled him. He jumped to his feet, almost upsetting his coffee, and glimpsed a flash of pale gray fur and tail before the thing disappeared. Running to the door, Siggerson peered out and saw the creature sitting in the corridor perhaps twenty feet away.

It came up to about his knees and had a sturdy, compact body slumped upon wide haunches. Its front legs almost resembled arms, for it hugged them loosely about itself. A long tail, covered in silky fur and twitching nervously, curled upon the floor. It had a round head with blue eyes set wide apart, shaggy little ear flaps that were pulled flat at the moment, and a short blunt muzzle.

Siggerson stared in astonishment. His anger faded away. This wasn't some scroungy pet smuggled aboard; it looked like a ouoji. Native to Minza and, according to old ship traditions, kept aboard for good luck, ouojis were reputedly highly intelligent. They had also become scarce, even rare. He found it hard to believe one had been put on the *Valiant* by the Minzanese shipwrights in these days of trying to preserve the species from extinction. But it was here, and there could be no other source for it.

Moving slowly so as not to startle the creature, he crouched and held out his hand. "Hungry?" he asked softly.

The blue eyes regarded him gravely, showing not fear but caution. To his surprise, Siggerson found himself talking to it as though it could understand him.

"I'm the pilot of this ship," he said. "I didn't understand about you, but you're a ouoji, aren't you, boy? You're a good luck piece. No wonder we got through those asteroids without a dent."

The ouoji opened his ear flaps, giving him a comical look of enquiry. He chittered softly and took a couple of tentative steps forward, tail lashing.

"Are you hungry?" asked Siggerson. "You can share my supper."

Carefully, making no sudden moves, he rose and walked back into the galley. He found a second plate and scraped half his portion onto it. Putting it on the floor about three feet away from himself, he went back to eating.

The ouoji came at last and sat in the doorway for a while, just watching. Then he went to the plate and sat down on his plump haunches. Picking up the plate with his front paws, he began to pick out the vegetables and eat them. He ate neatly but rapidly and was finished by the time Siggerson swallowed his last bite.

"Through?" Siggerson reached down and grasped the plate which the ouoji still held. It met his gaze and released the plate. Disconcerted by its obvious intelligence, Siggerson thoughtfully went through clean up. His response to the creature puzzled him. Normally he felt no attraction for pets. They were sentimental encumbrances, requiring too much care and attention. But the ouoji was different.

On impulse he went to his cabin and activated his vid for access to library data. Just as he found the entry for ouojis, however, his door opened.

Startled, Siggerson jumped and whirled around. But only the ouoji stood there. Siggerson swallowed. He hadn't realized it was large enough to activate the automatic doors. It chittered at him and turned as though to leave.

Siggerson wondered if it should be confined. Still, it had had run of the ship for days without any incidents other than a few stolen food packets. He turned back to the vid.

The ouoji chittered again, louder this time. Siggerson looked at it and it lashed its tail.

"If you want to play, forget it," said Siggerson.

The ouoji's blue eyes stared at him for a moment, then it came into his quarters. It bounced up and down on its forelegs and turned toward the door. Looking back at him, it chittered insistently.

Siggerson got to his feet in annoyance. "Okay, what is it?"

The ouoji ran for the door, paused again, and glanced back. Suppressing a sigh, Siggerson followed it. Satisfied, the ouoji streaked ahead down the corridor, heading aft. Reaching a ladder, it climbed with a competence that surprised Siggerson. On the top deck they headed toward the engines. Siggerson wondered if it had its lair in this area.

Instead, the ouoji scampered straight toward a check systems panel and bounced beneath it, chittering. With a frown, Siggerson pushed activation and at once the readout screen flashed warning red lights.

"A leak!" he said aloud, opening the panel hurriedly.

Within seconds he had the problem traced. A coolant line had begun seeping, probably due to the stress laid on during his race through the asteroid belt. It should have shown a warning on his master panel. As soon as Siggerson got back with the ship, Mohatsa would have to check the circuits for that glitch . . .

Siggerson looked up from his work in startlement, realizing where his thoughts were taking him. He glanced down at the ouoji, and those brilliant blue eyes seemed to shine with approval. Siggerson knew then that he wasn't going to steal the *Valiant*. He'd never had any real intention of doing so. It was just a momentary temptation. He would go back for the others. Anything else was inconceivable.

In the meantime, he had a leak to fix, thanks to the ouoji.

"Well, boy," he said, "you just paid for your supper. Thanks."

Kelly hung like a slab of meat by his fusion shackles in the unlit, unheated confines of the guardhouse. A few feet away, 41 dangled in a similar position. What it was doing to his burned arm, Kelly had no way of knowing. But 41 hadn't made a sound or a motion in the past two hours. Kelly hoped he was unconscious.

The door opened, and a blaze of sunlight blinded Kelly. Squinting, he glared at the guards silhouetted in the doorway.

"Hey!" he shouted. "It's about time you checked on us. Your pharaon agreed to abide by the rules of the Realto Convention. That includes granting medical care and food to prisoners—"

"Silence, *vasweem*," growled one of the guards. He strode inside with a swirl of his cloak and took up a position with his blaster drawn. Kelly noticed his cheek was bandaged; he'd probably sustained injury in the shelling.

Two more guards entered, pushing a pair of prisoners ahead of them. One was tall; one was short. Kelly squinted, trying to make them out better.

"Commander!" cried Phila Mohatsa. "You're alive!"

A weight inside Kelly suddenly lifted. He looked first at Phila, then at Beaulieu a step behind her. Both women were disheveled and muddy. They wore shackles, and their faces were grainy with fatigue. But they were alive. He grinned at them.

"You made it. I thought all hands went down with the ship."

Phila shook her head so that her unruly hair bounced. "We cleared just before . . . just before . . ." Her voice trailed off and she frowned.

The guards shoved them over by a wall. "Barbarian women should keep silent," snarled one.

Kelly twisted on his hook, grimacing at the pain in his arms and shoulders. He tried to read the expressions of the guards, wondering when they were going to take him to his first session with the mind sieve. Instead, two of the guards manhandled the unconscious 41 off his hook and dropped him on the ground.

"Hey!" shouted Kelly furiously.

Beaulieu took a step forward, but she was shoved back.

"Cause no trouble! Or we deal with him now." And the guard aimed his blaster at 41's skull.

Swallowing his rage, Kelly held back his protests. The guard poked at 41 with his toe, but 41 did not stir.

"Abomination," said the guard. "Half-breeds are strangled at birth."

"Not now," said another guard sharply.

They pulled Kelly down and dropped him with an equal lack of ceremony. He staggered but managed to keep from falling. One shoved him, and he dropped to his knees. His shoulders felt as though they had been wrenched from the socket. He bit his lip to keep from groaning.

The guards switched on one porta-lamp and a heater that puffed out weak warmth. They left food and a pail of ice-crusted water. Then they left, except for the burly trooper who had entered first. Holding his blaster in the crook of his arm, he positioned himself by the door and stared at them with stony indifference.

Gathering around the heater, Kelly, Phila, and Beaulieu shared quick, small smiles. Beaulieu touched Kelly's shoulder.

"How long have you been hanging like that?"

"Two hours."

"Much pain?"

Her hands were competent, pressing gently on tender spots. Kelly caught his breath. "Some." He shrugged away. "41 needs your attention more. He has a bad blaster burn and infection."

Beaulieu glanced at 41 with a frown. She still looked poised and elegant despite the dirt on her dark face. Phila, on the other hand, looked like a street urchin off some unregulated world.

"Who is this man?" asked Beaulieu as she bent over 41.

"A mercenary. He got my sister out of the mines and we've saved each other's lives a couple of times. We broke out of here together once, but we crashed in the hills and got brought back. He's trustworthy."

"He looks Salukan," said Phila doubtfully. "What did you call him?"

"41. He hasn't explained why he goes by a number instead of a name." Kelly hesitated. "He isn't receptive to many questions."

Beaulieu looked up with a frown. "He is in serious need of attention. These wounds have been neglected too long." She sighed. "Those bastards took my medikit. We can pull him closer to the heater and try to get some liquid down him." She hesitated, then pulled up her sleeve and peeled away a strip of flesh-colored adhesive from the inside of her forearm. Beneath it were two slim packets about the size of Kelly's thumbnail.

"This is my little personal emergency kit," said Beaulieu gruffly. "A mild antibiotic and painkiller. But I guess he needs it more than I do."

When 41 had been wrapped in Kelly's cloak and resettled, Kelly glanced at the guard. His translator gleamed upon his chest.

"All right," said Kelly as softly as he could. "Report in full. What happened to the ship? What the hell went wrong with the shield?"

"Siggerson dropped it," said Beaulieu crisply. "He also switched off teleport for forty-five minutes during the most crucial moments of your assault."

"What?" said Kelly in disbelief.

"Oh, yes, Commander," said Phila. "I would like to get that *scatsi* in my hands. I'd—"

"Never mind that. Why, Doctor? He must have had a reason."

"Yes." Beaulieu glanced at the guard and lowered her voice to a deep whisper. "He was trying to activate the defense system. He lacked three minutes in succeeding when we were discovered."

"Damn," whispered Kelly.

Beaulieu nodded. "Exactly. It was a gamble that did not pay off."

"I'd like to pay him off—"

"Mohatsa," said Kelly in warning. "At the moment our efforts should be going into planning a means of escape."

Her dark eyes fell from his. "Yes, sir. We need to eliminate that guard. If I could get close enough—"

"No. 41 and I pulled that before. He probably has orders to shoot us if we take a step in his direction."

"Why are they keeping us, anyway?" asked Beaulieu, checking 41's pulse again. "I thought they didn't take prisoners."

"Usually they don't. I think they've been putting everyone they capture in the mines," said Kelly.

"Then when they come to take us there, they'll kill this man," said Beaulieu angrily.

Kelly felt anger too. "It's likely. Doctor, do you know anything about their mind sieve apparatus?"

Beaulieu blinked in obvious surprise. "It's only the most diabolical form of torture yet devised by a sentient civilization. Why?"

Kelly stared at his hands. "Do you know any techniques that can be used to resist it? Do you have any familiarity with how it works? Any information at all that could be useful?"

She stared at him with dawning horror. "They're going to use it on you. They've told you so."

"Yes." Kelly glanced at Phila, who had turned pale. "Would you divide the food, please? We'd better eat while we have the chance."

She choked. "How can you think of food—"

He gripped her shoulder. "I'm starving. I haven't eaten since yesterday. None of us can be at our best unless we take care of basic survival needs."

"That's right," said Beaulieu, trying to recover. "How long?"

Kelly shrugged.

"I don't know much technically," she said slowly, her brow furrowed. "People tend to get emotional so there's little factual information. However, as I understand it the object is to probe the memory centers of your temporal lobes. They begin by affecting the hypothalamus part of your diencephalon—"

"Hold it!" said Kelly in bewilderment. "Less technical detail, please."

Beaulieu raked him with an impatient glance. "The forebrain. The hypothalamus is the seat of emotions such as fear or anger. It acts with the reticular system of the medulla oblongata. The reticular system brings together information from the cerebellum and other parts of the brain. It also keeps the brain alert. By manipulating these areas, they can achieve something along the lines of a truth serum without putting the side effects of a drug into the bloodstream."

Kelly and Phila exchanged glances.

"You know how erratic serums can be," continued Beaulieu. "They cause slurred speech in some subjects, erratic heart rate in others. Sometimes they fail completely. The subject may have seizures—"

"So the machine is more reliable," said Kelly, prompting her back from her tangent.

"Yes. Unfortunately. In one sense it's kinder to the subject. However, the harm comes from the probes into the memory centers. The more the subject resists, the more harm is done. Scar tissue in the cerebral cortex is dangerous."

Kelly had trouble swallowing. His voice sounded scratchy as he said, "What effects? Temporary and permanent?"

"Memory loss. Disorientation. Hysteria." Beaulieu paused, her eyes dark with compassion. "Convulsions. Insanity. Death. Any or all of them. We haven't many documented case studies of survivors so I can't be more precise."

Kelly nodded. Somehow Beaulieu's clinical voice made it all sound even worse. Feeling winded, he sat there in silence.

Phila jumped to her feet. "There's got to be a way to get out of here!"

At once the guard came alert and aimed his blaster at her.

Kelly tugged at her wrist. "Sit down. Let's not cause trouble until we're ready to."

"But what are we going to do, Commander?" she asked in anguish. "Just give the order and I'll—"

"The first order is to keep your head," he said sharply. "The second order is to save yourselves. If that means going into the mines, then do it. The longer they let you live, the better your chances are."

"I suppose Baker is having a party with them," said Phila bitterly. "He—"

"Baker is dead," said Kelly.

Phila drew a sharp breath. "Ah, then there is some justice. You killed him?"

"I don't kill my own men, operative," snapped Kelly, a pulse leaping beneath his left eye.

She looked abashed. "Sorry, sir. I—I come from a place where vendetta is practiced. Not to is considered . . ." Her voice trailed off and she shook her head. "Just a barbaric colony world. Never mind."

"Where is your home world?" asked Beaulieu gently.

But Phila's face grew pinched and distrustful. She shook her head. "I don't talk about it. It's an unimportant place."

"I was born on Feedee's Folly," said Beaulieu in amusement. "It took me many years and all my Academy days to get over my embarrassment about that. But now it's just a place. Ignorant, stagnant, complacent, like many other colonies."

Phila nodded, glancing at Kelly and Beaulieu, but she volunteered nothing more.

41 groaned and muttered something in a language Kelly's translator did not handle. Beaulieu bent over him at once.

Kelly glanced at Phila. "Did you recognize what he said?"

"No. It came through as gibberish." Phila frowned and touched the underside of her jaw where her translator was implanted. "This is supposed to incorporate ninety languages and dialects."

41 was stirring despite Beaulieu's attempts to quieten him. He jerked away from her hand, and Kelly moved to his side.

"41," he said. "Easy. You're with friends. This is Dr. Beaulieu, my medic. And Phila Mohatsa. Just lie still and let the doc take care of you."

41's tawny eyes glowed bright with fever. For a moment Kelly thought he did not understand, but he sank back down. "Water," he said.

Phila dipped a cup of the now thawed water and handed it to Beaulieu who put it to his lips. He gulped thirstily, then closed his eyes in apparent exhaustion.

"That will help you," said Beaulieu. "The drugs will start

taking effect soon if we can keep him warm and quiet. Damn! If I had even one—''

The door slammed open, startling them all. Involuntarily Kelly rose to his feet. Guards entered with drawn weapons.

One of them pointed at Kelly. ''You! Come at once. No speaking.''

Kelly thought he had himself prepared for this. But for a moment his mind went white with fear. He wanted to run for it. But being shot in the back like a coward was not the way he meant to die. Somehow he forced his suddenly wooden legs to move forward.

An inarticulate sound from Beaulieu made him glance over his shoulder. The sight seemed to burn into his mind: 41, lying crumpled and helpless, Beaulieu's grave eyes trying to send him courage, small, dirty Phila looking like a tigress who wanted to fight for him. He managed a lopsided smile of farewell and walked to meet the guards.

12

The bitter wind made Kelly shiver as he crossed the complex with his armed escort. The refinery had been cleaned up, but slagged windows and the smell of smoke still bore testament to yesterday's battle. Kelly kept his emotions down and assessed the remaining contingent of troopers with a professional eye. Many were walking wounded. Tents had been set up to replace the barracks. No ore carriers were in operation today. Their small sting assault had done a lot of damage. Kelly wished it had done more.

"*Aret chese,*" said one of the guards, poking him in the back.

Obediently Kelly halted before two metal pipes which had been driven into the ground and stood about head height. Two men had been impaled upon them, both humans in civilian clothes. Their deaths were fresh. Blood still glistened upon the trampled snow beneath. Feeling sick, Kelly glanced at their contorted faces, but neither of them was Caesar.

The guards laughed, thumping him. "We caught them sneaking into the complex. Fools. They did not even know how to fight. They gave us poor sport."

Kelly glared at the troopers. "You call us barbarians. We don't torture people or kill them for sport."

The guards sneered. "No," said one. "You take prisoners and bury them alive in cells, locked away in degradation like animals for the rest of their lives. Go on!"

Kelly was shoved forward. Reaching the administrative building, he was taken upstairs direct to Chumiri's office. The minlord, resplendent in his plaited wig and a doublet of heavy, lustrous cloth embroidered with gold thread, scowled as Kelly entered.

''I ordered your execution once, *vasweem*,'' he said in gutteral Glish. ''You have caused me much trouble.''

Kelly grinned. ''That's my job.'' He sat down in a chair without permission. ''Now,'' he said, ''about this situation. You are here in violation of treaty. You have murdered company employees and abused the rest. You have stolen millions of credits worth of pyrillium—''

''Enough!'' Chumiri struck his desk in anger. ''This is not a board of inquiry—''

''Isn't it?''

''This planet is ours, if we choose to take it,'' said Chumiri. ''And you, little kuprat-eater, cannot stop us.''

Kelly decided to keep bluffing. Studying his nails, he said casually, ''Seems to me that we already have. Your cargo is floating in space right now.''

Chumiri jumped to his feet with an oath. ''You dare boast of that?''

''Why not? You'll never recover it now. You don't have time.''

''Time?'' Chumiri frowned suspiciously. ''You mean because of the ore freighters which will be coming—''

''No,'' said Kelly.

Chumiri smiled. ''We have plans for them.''

''Another floating booby trap like those starving refugees?''

Chumiri's smile broadened. ''Perhaps.''

Kelly kept waiting for Chumiri to boast of having destroyed the *Valiant*, but when Chumiri said nothing about it Kelly frowned. ''As for my ship—''

''Your ship? *Askanth!*'' Chumiri struck his desk. ''Very clever, your little ship with its devices to make it disappear.''

Kelly went cold. The Salukans weren't supposed to know about that development.

''We were supposed to think it was destroyed inside the asteroid belt. But we are not so easily fooled. The mailord will wait until it comes out, and then he will eliminate it.''

''The mailord will not do so,'' said a deep, cynical voice from the doorway.

Chumiri and the guards jerked to attention, and Kelly stared as the Salukan strolled into the office. He was the first true Salukan aristocrat Kelly had ever seen. He possessed the facial characteristics of a long nose and wide-set eyes which his lesser-bred officers attempted to paint on. Only the blue bars of warrior status adorned his cheeks. Beside him, Chumiri looked coarse and gaudy.

The mailord wore no wig at all, and his elongated skull was shaven and oiled to satin smoothness. His crimson cloak hung in voluminous folds off his shoulders, and silver threads embroidered the borders. He stripped off his jewel-encrusted gauntlets and flung them down. An attendant at his heels removed his cloak, and he stood in a doublet of ruby cloth unadorned except for his silver sash of office.

Like all Salukans, he honored tradition by carrying a dagger; his was a long one—almost the length of a forearm from hilt to tip in the style of the Genisset House. No doubt the hair lock of a revered ancestor had been fitted into the hilt, and it had probably been passed down from father to son for generations. Kelly's breath caught in admiration. Such a dagger was very rare for collectors. At the mailord's throat hung the Star of Pharaon, highest of Salukan military honors.

"The ship eluded us," said the mailord. He shrugged, snapping his fingers lightly, and the attendant fetched him something to drink. "I could have shot my captain and promoted another in his place, but the Alliance ship would still be gone."

He glanced at Kelly, taking in the bedraggled black uniform with eyes that were a surprising violet blue, like twilight. "You are the commander of this Special Operations endeavor?" he asked in flawless Glish.

"Yes," said Kelly.

The mailord inclined his head. "My compliments to your pilot. He put mine to shame."

"Mailord Duseath!" said Chumiri, finally recovering his powers of speech. "How . . . could there not be a . . . surely there is . . ."

"No." The mailord accepted his cup and drank deeply. "I see that in my absence you have not yet managed to recover the cargo now floating around this miserable planet."

Chumiri's cheeks darkened. "Not yet, mailord," he gasped.

The twilight eyes shifted to Kelly again. "How fast is your ship, Commander?"

Kelly smiled. "I really couldn't say."

Duseath acknowledged the parry with a flicker of a smile. "I estimate an emergency speed of time distort 11.1. My battlecruiser can achieve 11.058. It is interesting to observe the Alliance's latest technological developments. She could return to your nearest space station in three days? Or is it four? I do not recall the precise calculations you use in marking your days."

He turned to Chumiri. "Three days to go, three days to return. We have that long to finish here."

Chumiri saluted. "By Pharaon's will."

Duseath gestured with a slim hand. "What is your intention for the commander? I heard threats of execution as I entered. Are you that unimaginative, minlord?"

"No," said Chumiri. "The mind sieve first. I want to know the secrets of the concealment shield."

"Then an engineer should question him."

Kelly stood up to face the mailord. "Two members of my squad are prisoners. Do you intend to interrogate them as well?"

Duseath lifted his brows at Chumiri, who made a sound of scorn.

"Females, mailord."

"We have no interest in your women," said Duseath. "They will go into the mines."

Kelly kept his expression carefully neutral, not wanting to betray too much relief. Salukans seemed unable to grasp the idea of equality between the sexes. In this case, that was to Mohatsa's and Beaulieu's advantage.

Duseath snapped his fingers. "Take him out."

The guards closed in on Kelly. Desperately he threw out the only thing he had left.

"You're wrong if you think you have six days, son of Genisset."

There was a gasp from someone. Duseath gestured and the guards stepped back. "This human amuses me," he said. "How do you know my ancestor?"

Kelly smiled. "I collect daggers. I've studied all the designs. At least the major ones. I'm learning to recognize the minor houses and some of the tribes now.'' He shrugged. ''A little hobby of mine.''

''A barbarian who aspires to culture.'' Duseath looked surprised. ''You flatter us. Why am I wrong?''

The sudden switch of subject didn't throw Kelly. ''Because the *Wellington* is on her way here now.''

Both Duseath and Chumiri broke into laughter. ''Easily threatened,'' said Duseath. ''But our intelligence reports say she is undergoing repairs at Station 4.'' He smiled at Kelly's expression. ''Go on with him. *Uste!*''

As he went out, Kelly kept alert for the least sign of inattention that would give him a chance to break for it. But the guards flanked him tightly with their blasters drawn. Down the corridor, they entered what looked like a former conference room. It had been fitted with a metal chair surrounded by three squat cylinders connected to each other with flexible, transparent tubing. At the rear a small generator on a grav-flat hummed in readiness, and a sophisticated recording system was linked to a computer that probably supervised the whole apparatus.

One of the guards seized Kelly's forearm and held him with a tight grip while he unlocked the fusion shackles. Kelly tensed, but the other guard put his blaster about two inches from Kelly's face.

He was motioned to the metal chair. Gingerly Kelly sat down. At once metal restraints clamped his wrists and ankles. A wigless Salukan in a scientist's smock grasped Kelly's head from behind. A clamp fastened about Kelly's throat. The cold metal made him flinch.

Both guards relaxed, putting away their blasters and exchanging jokes with the scientist, who looked harried.

''Don't kill him too soon, Theptse. Look at his heartrate. Are humans always that slow? I've heard humans have their hearts just below the throat. Curious place.''

The scientist shooed them outside. Kelly swallowed with difficulty and watched the man at work hooking up monitors and increasing power from the generator.

''How long does this take?'' he asked.

Theptse glanced briefly at him, but made no answer. Kelly noticed he wore no translator slung about his neck. A screen came on, and Kelly saw himself projected there. He looked scared. He tried to draw a deep breath, but he couldn't. His heart raced faster and faster. Beaulieu's words returned to him: the more you resist, the more damage is done.

All right. He'd give them all the information he knew about the *Wellington*, hold her in his mind for as long as he could. There was nothing about battlecruiser specs they didn't know anyway. Then he'd . . .

Unexpected pain lanced through his skull. He jerked and grimaced, closing his eyes to fight it. Scarlet washed through his mind. Even the movement of his eyeballs behind his lids hurt. He gasped, drawing his head to one side. Nothing helped. He could not evade the relentless throb that went deeper and deeper into his brain. His fingers curled over the ends of the chair and tightened.

"No!"

His skull seemed to split wide open, and whiteness dazzled everything. He sat tensed, panting. The pain vanished, and for a moment he sat limp with relief. He hadn't had a migraine like that since . . . He realized suddenly that his mind was kaleidoscoping freely through memories and thoughts. Hastily he tried to shut them off.

The pain speared him again. This time he cried out, throwing himself against the restraints. Unendurable agony went on forever, until he lost consciousness of anything save that of the pain itself. It ended abruptly, and he sagged with a grateful sob. Once again it took him several seconds to come out of his daze and realize his mind was spilling all kinds of knowledge.

He cracked open his eyes a bit and saw a rapidly shifting collage of images flowing across the screen. In surprise he realized his thought stream was being recorded directly with no attempt at guidance or specific questions. Once recorded, the tape could be slowed down and specific bits of information isolated for prolonged study. There was no way to resist this.

Still, he tried thinking about the *Wellington*. At once the blurred images flashing across the screen began to slow fractionally.

The pain stabbed him more harshly than ever. He heard screaming and realized it was his own. Then even his awareness of that faded.

An unspecified number of minutes later, he came to, and found himself sobbing like a child. Again, as soon as he became cognizant, the images on the screen slowed. The scientist turned toward him, and Kelly yelled, "No! Please, not again."

At once he was ashamed of his own weakness and fear. He had been trained to resist interrogation. But nothing had prepared him for this.

Theptse glanced away. "The uninhibitors are now in place. We can begin."

Kelly went cold inside as his translator deciphered what the man was saying. He didn't think he could face much more of this, and according to Beaulieu's information he'd just come through the easy part. Swallowing, he turned his head as far as the throat clamp would allow to see who the scientist was talking to.

Duseath stood in the room, looking bored and impatient. He saw Kelly's gaze upon him and said, "I have decided to conduct the interrogation myself."

Kelly tried to speak and failed. He swallowed and tried again. "You mean you want more?"

"Of course. Military training and childhood memories . . . pah." He snapped his fingers in dismissal. "You are of the Special Operations branch of the Allied Intelligence Agency. You have mental protectors installed in your mind to protect classified knowledge. That is what I want."

Kelly's mouth dried out. "You can't," he whispered. "They can't be broken."

Duseath smiled. "Yes, they can." He gestured at Theptse. "Begin."

Kelly tensed, waiting for the terrible pain. Instead, a low vibration shook his skull, penetrating his brain. At first he was wary, then he relaxed a fraction, thinking he could endure this. Imperceptibly, however, the vibration increased until his head felt like it was being shaken apart. He gritted his teeth, telling himself he could handle it, focusing his mind on the *Wellington.* She would come soon and blast the wigheads to eternity.

"Very good," said Duseath's voice in Glish. "Your name and rank."

That was easy. Kelly hurried to answer, then frowned and hesitated.

The vibration increased, almost driving him mad. ''Name and rank,'' repeated Duseath.

''Comdr. Bryan Kelly, serial number 400659.''

''The prefix 400 specifies Intelligence.''

''Yes.'' Kelly could not seem to hold back the word.

''The digit 6?''

''Sixth fleet—''

''Wrong!'' Pain speared Kelly. ''Sixth fleet is Minzanese.''

As soon as the pain dropped, Kelly dragged in a breath.

''The digit 6?'' said Duseath.

''Code . . . for Jedderson.''

''Fleet Admiral Jedderson?''

''Yes.''

''You remain under his jurisdiction?''

Everything military was. Kelly hesitated, fearing the pain again. ''Yes.''

''The digit 5?''

''M-my division.''

Duseath said nothing. Something in Kelly struggled to keep speaking, to fill the silence. He tried to resist and lost.

''Peregrine Division. Squad Alpha.''

''How many divisions in Special Operations?''

''F-four.''

''Why is it coded with the numeral 5?''

''I don't know,'' said Kelly.

The pain caught him hard and seemed to go on and on until he thought he would die. When it ended, he was dripping with sweat. Panic filled him. If that pain came again . . .

''Why—''

''There were originally five divisions,'' said Kelly hastily. Shame at his own fear made the words taste sour. ''One folded.''

''The digit 9?''

''Meaningless. Wait,'' said Kelly quickly. ''It—it is a trigger code to the number suffix.''

''Which is?''

''773.''

''Explain.''

"My personal identification number," said Kelly, his voice shaking at this first actual breach of classification.

"Interpret transmission code Karen Betty Alice."

Little twitches ran through Kelly. Protests rose inside him, but he could not stop himself. "Transmission Code KBA is current for scrambled messages between AIA headquarters and all base operations."

"What is the frequency?"

Kelly drew a blank. He shivered, waiting for punishment. The pain did not strike. That seemed more frightening. Deep inside him a voice seemed to be saying, "No, Kelly. Be silent."

"What is the frequency?"

He felt that if he failed to answer, Duseath would kill him and that if he *did* answer he would go insane. Perhaps if he broke the protector and gave Duseath what he wanted, Duseath would be satisfied and end this.

"What is the frequency?"

Kelly drew a ragged breath, aware that he must not break. If he gave way now, this easily, he was unworthy of his rank, of his service, of his father.

The humming vibration increased, creating an itch inside his brain that was maddening. He wanted to tear his hands free of the clamps and get to it, but he couldn't.

"What is the frequency?"

"Please," he whispered. *"Please."*

"What is the frequency?"

Hold on, he told himself desperately. *Don't give the bastard anything.*

A dart of pain like a needle touched him. He screamed.

"Too much," said Theptse in warning. "You're going to shatter him too soon."

"You said no protectors could resist," snarled Duseath. "Again!"

"Mailord—"

"Again!"

Hold on, Kelly told himself.

The pain came like a wave this time, washing such agony over him he could neither scream nor move. And in a far, dim corner of his brain it occurred to him that nothing was worth this. No amount of loyalty and no amount of pride.

He gritted his teeth, lost in the agony. It *was* worth it. It had to be, or his whole life and all he had striven to become was a joke. The lives of his squad would have been given for nothing, and ruthless invaders like Duseath and Chumiri would grind freedom beneath their heels.

"Mailord," said Theptse in warning.

"Continue!"

Kelly writhed against the restraints. He was screaming now, and that did not shame him. But his fear built inside him, and he did not want to die like this. He did not want to spend the rest of his life gibbering in an asylum. And the blackness was coming closer. He fought it, screaming louder, aware that once the blackness engulfed him he would be broken and Duseath could play freely with the contents of his mind. He had to speak; he had to overcome the protector which pounded against him in response to the pain.

"What is the frequency?"

"121!" he said, gasping. Sweat drenched him. The restraints cut into his wrists as he fought to speak. He tried to look at Duseath, but he could not open his eyes enough to see through the haze of pain engulfing him. "The f-frequency is 121."

There. It was out. He shuddered, feeling himself stretched to the breaking point.

"Ah. I believe I see. Every five letters of your alphabet repeats the pattern. How simple."

Pain and vibration faded together, leaving Kelly trembling weakly in the chair. With difficulty he opened his eyes, waiting for Theptse to catch the lie. Then they would shatter him without mercy.

The room blurred around him, but he managed to bring it back into focus. He looked at Duseath, who was watching Theptse fiddle with his equipment.

"Well?" demanded Duseath. Kelly held his breath.

Theptse shook his head. "No clear reading, mailord. But with pain that intense, lying becomes almost impossible."

Duseath hissed with impatience and whirled on Kelly, who flinched. "Lies or truth? I do not trust you, Commander."

Kelly wanted to tell Duseath what he could do with his distrust. Instead, he forced himself to express the fear his own nature wanted to hide.

"Please," he whispered. "Not again."

"Ah. Now you respect us a little. You haven't yet learned what pain is, Commander." Duseath thumped his abdomen, where his knuckles rapped hollowly on the bony plate that protected his heart. "We learn the realities of life from birth. Childhood is a time of testing and toughening our minds and bodies. We must be strong to live, stronger than the rest. We learn to welcome pain, for it strengthens us. We do not fear it. But, you. Ah, yes." He peered close into Kelly's eyes, and at that proximity Kelly could see the dish and curve of the bones in his skull, the long teeth that resembled fangs, the odd set of those merciless eyes in their sockets.

"You," said Duseath softly, "are afraid. That is because you are weak. You have not learned to conquer fear. Each day of your miserable, puny existence you battle it because it is untamed. I have read the literature of your people. You call fear many names in an attempt to hide it. Conscience, loyalty, love. Pah. How many deaths lie on your blame? You are a warrior. You lead men. How many have you sent to their deaths? Can you remember their names, their faces, their number?"

Appalled, unable to evade that relentless gaze, Kelly frowned back at him. "I remember," he said hoarsely.

Duseath drew back slightly. "It is said that humans cannot keep themselves from lying, but that they feel guilty afterward until they must confess. Is this true?"

"Sometimes," said Kelly, sweating. From the corner of his eye he could see Theptse hovering over the monitors. It was all he could do not to glance at the scientist.

"Yours is a confused people. I wonder how they live with themselves. Why did you give me that frequency, Commander? Why didn't you hold out?"

Kelly stared at him, not daring to answer.

Duseath snorted. "Is it the operational frequency?"

Kelly hesitated. "I heard my commanding officer order it to be used."

Duseath glanced at Theptse, then back at Kelly. "You evade me."

"You don't expect me to just babble on and on in cooperation, do you?" said Kelly with exasperation. "The traitor

Baker was willing to do that. If you want answers from me, you'll have to yank them out by force."

"I intend to," said Duseath.

Despite himself, Kelly felt the hairs on his arms stand up. Just the thought of going through another session of the mind sieve was enough to make dread twist inside him.

"Is the frequency current?" snapped Duseath. "Yes or no?"

"Yes!" retorted Kelly. He thought then that it was over. The monitor would either determine that his heart and respiration rates were too ragged and sound an alarm, or his efforts to sound increasingly angry before this answer would trick it. He waited, holding his breath.

Duseath glanced at Theptse, who shrugged. Duseath sighed.

"Very well, Commander. It seems you have spoken the truth. And you have not died from this invasion of your mental conditioning, and you are not insane. Interesting. You are a puzzle to me. I find myself curious, yet despite Theptse's wondrous machine, my doubts of you remain."

Kelly's relief was too intense to hide. He averted his face. "Maybe I'm not a shining example of Special Operations," he mumbled.

Duseath grasped his chin and turned his face. "Is it shame you feel, barbarian? Shame of the beaten? Shame of the defeated? You spout brave words, but beneath that defiance quakes a little man. Hah!"

He released Kelly and strode away, leaving the imprint of his nails to sting Kelly's skin. Kelly drew in a breath and briefly closed his eyes. He felt drained of energy. *Please, let it be over.*

Theptse came and released the restraint clamps. For a moment Kelly thought he could not sit up without them.

"You have done well, Commander," said Duseath. "Now that you have broken through the first barrier, the others will be easier. Rest and then we shall begin again."

Kelly stared at him in dismay. "You don't have enough?"

Duseath laughed. "There is never enough." He pulled one of the comm/teleport wristbands from his pocket and held it up for Kelly to see. "Your link with your ship, I believe. You cannot disappear into the air without it. This theory of displaced physics—you humans call it teleportation, our spies say, and the Minzanese call it place-jumping, so quaint, your allies—will soon join our usable technology, but your information on the matter will be useful.''

''I'm no engineer,'' retorted Kelly. ''You can torture me all day long and never learn how that works.''

Duseath sighed. ''Your understanding is on the level of a child's. I will ask you about how you deploy troop movements with the use of this. How you time yourself. How you keep track of troops on the battlefield and how they are recalled. Those questions you can answer.''

Kelly set his mouth stubbornly.

Duseath laughed and opened the door to leave. ''You *will* answer. Reconcile yourself to it. You belong to us now.''

13

Before Duseath could leave, however, a young officer came running up to him and stood panting.

"Mailord!" he said in urgent Saluk. "Priority dispatch from your ship."

Duseath frowned and put forth a hand to the boy. "Wait for me in the minlord's office. I shall be there presently—"

"Forgive me, mailord. It cannot wait." The youth gulped a little, then plunged ahead. "Long-range communications scan has picked up a transmission from the Earth ship *Wellington*."

Kelly came out of his chair, and Duseath threw him a startled glance before seizing the officer's shoulder.

"Speak fully. How far away?"

"It is traveling at a constant speed of TD 8. If that is maintained, it will reach Chealda within twenty-two hours."

Duseath paled. "In Askanth's name!" he swore. "Is nothing to favor us on this wretched planet?"

Relief flooded Kelly. The hangar chief and mechanics at Station 4 must have worked a miracle to get her ready this soon. He smiled. "You were warned."

Duseath scowled and uttered something that Kelly's translator failed to interpret. "I wish to speak to the communications officer. Open a link and inform the minlord of this. I want him to join me at once."

The young officer saluted. "Yes, mailord."

Duseath snapped his fingers. "Guards!"

They stepped in as the youth hurried out. Duseath pointed at Kelly. "Bring him."

The guards closed in on Kelly, but this time he was glad of their proximity. His legs felt shaky, and he had a sense of unreality as though he floated through a dream. Yet he knew this was reality. His friend Tso Marks served under an able young captain on the *Wellington.* Marks had told Kelly that Captain Ferraro was tough and aggressive in a fight.

Downstairs, the Salukan staff and adjutants clustered about the comm. They scattered at Duseath's arrival, and the operator opened a ground/ship link. Kelly looked at the small viewscreen, but to his disappointment it was not activated. He had hoped to catch a glimpse of the cruiser's flightdeck to describe later to Commodore West's research data boys.

"*Hut eth saluent a bativere* Emis Devuet. Greetings and respect given to the battleship *Emis Devuet,*" said Duseath impatiently.

The disembodied reply came back with equal formality: "Greetings and long health to the mailord."

Duseath snorted and shifted his feet. "Your report on the earth ship now approaching . . . any change?"

"Negative, mailord."

"You have definitely established that her course is toward us? She is not on random patrol of this quadrant?"

"Negative, mailord. Her course runs true. Her transmissions activity with the other ship indicate that she is not on patrol."

The Salukans glanced at each other in sudden silence. Chumiri came hurrying down the stairs and joined them as Duseath said quietly, "What other ship? Specify."

"Non-coded transmissions per rendezvous instructions with Minzanese ship *Omu Donde.*"

Duseath's head whipped around. He stalked toward Kelly, who stood there grinning at their consternation.

"You!" snapped Duseath in Glish. "Information on these ships."

At least a dozen pairs of hostile eyes regarded Kelly. He faced them all, projecting as much confidence as he could.

"Sure," he said with a shrug. "But you already know about the *Wellington.* She's a heavy-class battlecruiser with more victories notched on her record than any other ship in the combined fleets. The *Omu Donde* is a light cruiser, built for speed and weaponry. She'll outmaneuver your old tub without—''

''Idle boasting,'' said Chumiri with a scowl. He flung his tan cloak over his shoulder and glared at Duseath. ''Why listen to the words of this kuprat-eater? He seeks to make us afraid.''

''You thought you had six days to clear out,'' said Kelly. ''Now you have a few hours. The odds are two to one. Maybe three to one. After all, you don't know where my ship is.''

''Your ship,'' sneered Chumiri. ''Your ship is a gnat. A nothingness.''

''Silence,'' said Duseath sharply. ''You contribute nothing.''

Chumiri shrugged. ''This last freighter is of small importance. The others are halfway to the empire borders with enough pyrillium for this year. Let us go from this miserable place.''

Duseath nodded. ''There must be no one left to speak of us. Those are our orders.''

Chumiri bared his stained teeth. ''The will of the mailord is done. I'll give the order to gas the mines immediately.''

Shock drained through Kelly. He took a step forward, only to have a guard seize his arm. ''What?'' he said. ''You mean kill the civilians? All of them? But why?''

Duseath looked at him as though he were a naive child, then turned away without a word. ''Orderly departure drills,'' he said to a nodding oparch. ''Let the camps be struck cleanly. There must be no identifying proof of our presence.''

''What about Hamar and the refugees on that freighter?'' said Kelly angrily. ''They've already identified you—''

''Sick people, hallucinating, hysterical?'' Duseath snorted. ''They may mew and moan, but they will turn on anyone who seeks to help them. That will destroy their credibility. And there will be no proof to justify what they say.'' He smiled. ''Without proof, there can be no war.''

''Don't count on it,'' said Kelly grimly.

Chumiri shouted with laughter. ''The little hawk shrieks for battle. Listen to him flutter his wings. Oh, you frighten us, *vasweem*.''

''Our pharaon knows the mind of your leaders,'' said Duseath. "The Alliance does not want war now. It will not seek an excuse to wage one. Meanwhile, we are richer, and I go home to a triumph in the streets and the approbation of my ruler."

Chumiri's mockery and Duseath's cruel satisfaction appalled Kelly. His pulse kicked hard in his temple. His headache came back, but he forced himself to ignore it.

Chumiri laughed at him and came over, waving Kelly's guards aside. "You have a sickness, *vasweem*?" he mocked. "A sickness of defeat? Your ugly face shines like paste. Tell me, is it the death of these miners which turns your stomach, or the idea of your own execution?"

Giving Kelly a shove, he strode away. Kelly stared after him with a rising sense of desperation. He had to stop the executions now. And there was only one way to do it.

Gathering all his strength, he sprang past his inattentive guards and tackled Duseath from behind. The mailord lost his balance and fell sprawling with Kelly on top of him. Tangled together in the billowing folds of Duseath's crimson cloak, they grappled fiercely. Kelly pinned Duseath's arms behind him. Duseath managed to pull one arm free. Cursing in Saluk, he twisted in Kelly's hold, but Kelly straddled the mailord and used his weight to hold him down. Duseath struggled, trying to dislodge Kelly.

Aware that he couldn't match Duseath strength for strength in his weakened condition, Kelly seized the ceremonial dagger from Duseath's belt and pressed it against the mailord's throat.

At once Duseath froze, his eyes widening and his face taking on a slight sheen. "Well?" he grunted. "Kill me now and go to your gods a hero."

Kelly ignored him and glared at the hostile faces surrounding him. "Keep back!" he ordered. "Or I cut his throat."

The troopers slowly backed up. They parted for Chumiri, who came hurtling through. His weathered face looked thunderous with rage. "You fool! Release the mailord. Now! You cowardly little—"

"Shut up," said Kelly in the coldest voice he could muster. "There will be no more murders. No one else on Chealda is going to die. Except your mailord if you carry out his orders."

Chumiri scowled and started to protest.

"No!" said Kelly. "You especially, minlord. If you give the word, his death is on you." For emphasis, Kelly pressed the sharp blade more tightly to Duseath's sleek throat. Duseath twitched in pain. Chumiri's knotted brows showed that he saw it.

"I will kill you, *vasweem*, if you do not let him go."

Kelly shook his head. "You've already promised my execution no matter what. I have nothing to lose. You, minlord, have everything to lose. Now, release those people from the mines."

Chumiri hesitated, glancing from Kelly to the mailord. Duseath said nothing. His breathing was audible, unsteady.

"Mailord?" asked Chumiri at last. Although his tone was humble, his eyes blazed hatred at Kelly.

Duseath started to speak, but with a jerk Kelly stopped him.

"You don't need his orders; you have mine. What's it to be?"

Chumiri swallowed. He glanced at the other troopers and officers as if to gauge their reactions. "I will release them. Wait a moment."

He started to walk away, but Kelly called after him, "If you try that trick, you'll regret it. Give the order from here, where I can hear what you say."

Muttering, Chumiri turned back and took a communicator from a worried-looking oparch. He gave the orders to release the miners, cutting off any exclamations of surprise from the overseers. Switching off the comm, he glared at Kelly.

"Does this satisfy you?"

"Not yet. Release my squad."

Chumiri's eyes narrowed, but he turned in silence and nodded to one of his oparchs. "Bring them here."

The officer left the building. Kelly stared at the Salukans who remained. "Back away. If any of you tries something, he dies."

Five endless minutes later, the oparch returned. With him came Beaulieu, Phila, a shaky-looking 41, Kevalyn, Caesar, and another man Kelly did not recognize. The troopers moved aside in a block to make way for them. Hostility tightened the air.

Caesar, his red hair standing up in an unruly thatch, looked like he'd been run over by an ore carrier. He grinned ruefully at Kelly. "Sorry, Boss," he said. "We were supposed to be rescuing you or saving the day or something."

It wasn't much of a joke, but Kelly was too glad to see Caesar alive to care. His gaze went to Kevie.

She looked thinner than when he'd last seen her. Thinner and a little worn, but still resilient and beautiful. Still his big sis, who couldn't get along with the old man except at a distance, who never came home to create peace in the family. She returned his gaze with a searching one of her own; he nodded, and she tried to smile at him without much success.

"The resistance," said Chumiri with scorn, prodding her. "When women go to war, their army is one of cowards and fools: easily caught, easily broken."

Kevalyn jerked away from his touch. Blindness swept over Kelly. His hold on Duseath tightened, and the mailord grunted in pain. Kelly glanced down and saw a fine beading of dark blood appear along the knife blade. Duseath's dark blue eyes remained locked on his. For the first time their gaze held fear combined with respect. He believed Kelly would kill him.

A stir went around the room. "Blood," whispered someone. "The *vasweem* has taken the mailord's blood."

Chumiri whipped out his blaster. "Now we have what you Earthers call a stalemate."

"Back off!" said Kelly angrily. "You and your men leave your weapons and go to the other side of the room. We'll—"

A mutter rose among the troopers. Chumiri scowled. "Oh, no, it is not that easy. We are not spineless worms to twist and squirm to your bidding."

Tired and exasperated, Kelly snapped, "Enough rhetoric. We all know how brave you are. But it's over. You're finished here. Now—"

"If you believe we will meekly surrender just because you threaten our mailord, you deceive yourself. You have accomplished nothing. Without the specific password of the day, no order given over a communicator is obeyed in enemy territory. The *vasweemi* in the mines will still be gassed."

Kelly gritted his teeth. He should have caught that trick. His mind was still a bit fuzzy from the mind sieve, but now . . . He frowned. "I still have the mailord."

Chumiri grunted. "And I have your friends. If he dies, they die. What is to be done?"

The situation had gone from bad to rotten. The smugness in Chumiri's voice made Kelly determined not to betray his worry. He shrugged. "Big talk, minlord. But I can wait here all day long until the *Wellington* and *Omu Donde* arrive. How long do you want to wait?"

Chumiri scowled. Kelly relaxed a fraction, thinking he had the wily minlord at last. But without warning, Chumiri turned and fired on the man standing beside Kevalyn.

She screamed. "Rege! My God, no!"

The man staggered back, surprise frozen on his face as he crumpled to the floor.

"One down," said Chumiri while Kelly crouched there in rage and shock. Chumiri pointed his blaster at Kevalyn. Her eyes widened and she stared at the weapon as though mesmerized. "You created the game," said Chumiri to Kelly. "How long do we play it?"

Sickened and enraged, Kelly forced himself to get over his shock quickly. He looked at Kevalyn, anguished by the decision he had to make. Could he justify surrendering just to save her? Personal considerations did not, could not outweigh his duty. The service would not stand for it. And yet how could he sacrifice her—or Caesar, Beaulieu, Phila, and 41—to save everyone else on this planet?

Unbidden, the haunting screams of his previous squad came back to him. He saw their deaths again, agony splashed upon their faces because of his split-second lapse in judgment. No error had been blamed on him in the inquiry, but he blamed himself. He always would. And now, to face it again, to defy these butchers who would mow down his people, one by one, in front of him, unless he surrendered . . .

And if he did surrender, the Salukans would kill them all just the same.

Anger hardened Kelly. He met Kevie's gray eyes. She shook her head, telling him not to surrender. His gaze swept past her to Caesar's white face, set with stubbornness. To little Phila Mohatsa, who looked scared and angry and defiant. To Beaulieu, who had on that expression of clinical detachment which doctors wear when they're about to impart bad news. To 41, who should not even be involved, yet was glaring at Chumiri and that blaster aimed at Kevalyn as though nothing else in the world existed. Something sore and tight loosened a bit inside Kelly; these were good operatives, sound people. He had chosen them well.

"Your bluff has been called," said Duseath very, very quietly against the knife. He had pulled his free hand up against his chest. "The fear we spoke of earlier, it keeps you from killing in *que'se ta dyt*? Cold blood? Yes, you humans fear that very much."

Kelly frowned. "Go to hell," he said. "You—"

Duseath shifted beneath Kelly, rolling from his side onto his back. His free hand flashed at Kelly with a tiny knife, pulled from concealment in his clothing.

Kelly dodged, felt Duseath almost twist free, and desperately slashed with his own dagger. Dark blood spurted across Kelly's hand, and the wet stench of it filled his nostrils, choking him.

Duseath's throat, however, was protected by hard cartilage beneath the thin layer of skin and muscle. Yelling in pain, he stabbed at Kelly, who felt a sharp sting along his arm. Duseath broke free and struck Kelly across the temple with his forearm. The blow was numbing. Kelly toppled back, and Duseath twisted to his feet.

At once guards pounced on Kelly. One wrested the dagger from his grasp. They hauled him up, shaking him between them, and held him fast.

Breathless and groggy, Kelly shook his head clear. He saw his squad surrounded by armed troopers. Caesar looked murderous. He shot Kelly an inquiring glance. Kelly grimaced that he was all right.

Duseath dabbed at his bleeding throat with a cloth. His thin face blazed with anger. There was no mercy, no compassion at all in his eyes. "You're a fool," he said. "If you had killed me, they would have respected you. You would have died honorably and quickly. But there is nothing more shameful than a commander who fails. Now, see how your people will die."

He gestured curtly, and Chumiri's blaster leveled on Kevalyn.

Kelly heard her gasp of fear, and he tried to shove past the guards. "Damn you, *no*!"

He could not get through. 41, however, sprang at her in a blur, knocking her sprawling just as Chumiri fired. The sound filled the room and echoed in Kelly's ears. He stood there immobile, unable to breathe, seeing over and over again in his mind Kevalyn going down.

"Kevie," he whispered.

But she wasn't dead. On the floor, 41 and Kevalyn untangled themselves and slowly sat up. Kelly stared, first at them then at the blackened mark on the wall where Chumiri had missed. Kelly's lungs felt flattened as though they could never inflate again.

But as his shock faded, rage took its place. He realized from the smirk on Chumiri's face that the minlord had intended to miss. Clenching his fists, Kelly glared past the troopers at Chumiri. "You—"

The minlord turned away and motioned Kevalyn aside. White-faced, she scrambled toward Caesar, who helped her to her feet.

"Even ugly human women have amusement to offer," said Chumiri.

Kelly stiffened, but Kevalyn faced Chumiri with more anger than fear.

"Go ahead and gloat," she said. "You're nothing but a bully occupied with childish games of proving your own machismo by trying to intimidate us."

Chumiri's weathered face darkened with fury. Without answering, he aimed his blaster at 41, who still sat on the floor. "Well, savior of loud-mouthed women? Why were you not strangled at birth?"

41 did not seem perturbed by the insults. He said something quietly in Saluk which did not translate to Kelly.

A trooper sniggered. Chumiri stiffened, and Kelly thought he would shoot 41. Instead, he motioned with his blaster. "Get up, abomination, and face your death."

Instead of complying, 41 launched himself at Chumiri's knees, sending the minlord sprawling. Someone shouted in anger. Kelly seized advantage of the momentary confusion to slap aside one blaster and double up another trooper with a well-placed punch to the soft part of his chest. He slung the gasping trooper into the men who rushed him.

Chumiri had 41 by the throat. Kelly kicked Chumiri hard

in the side, and with a shout the minlord fell sprawling. 41 wriggled free, seizing the blaster from Chumiri's hand. Together he and Kelly ran for it, yelling at the rest of the squad to follow.

A shot scorched over Kelly's head and blasted the door ahead of him. He skidded to one side, diving in a roll that brought him up against the wall. The blaster in his hand kicked with a swift series of recoils as he fired back. Two more troopers went down. Nearby, 41 had dived for cover behind the sprawled body of a trooper and was shooting with deadly precision.

"Outside!" yelled Kelly.

He continued to lay down covering fire, using the blaster on continuous bursts in a reckless expenditure of the charge. At this rate, his blaster would be exhausted soon. Longing for a fleet-issue Maxell bi-muzzle pistol, Kelly went on firing, sweeping the room as troopers scattered and took cover behind overturned work tables.

Return fire was erratic, either wide or close enough to make him flinch. After several seconds Kelly realized the troopers were deliberately aiming to miss.

"Boss!" yelled Caesar.

From his peripheral vision Kelly saw Caesar ducking outside behind the women. Kelly glanced at 41 and motioned for him to follow. 41 pulled himself to a quick crouch and ran for it, while Kelly covered him. Then it was Kelly's turn.

He scrambled to his feet and headed for the door. This was the tricky part, shooting while he ran. But as he reached the stone steps outside, his blaster jammed. He squeezed the trigger again before realizing the charge had drained. Tossing it aside, Kelly jumped in a long dive and hit the steps with bruising impact, rolling with an impetus that banged his knees and elbows.

A hand grabbed his arm and jerked him to one side. It was Beaulieu. Kelly gripped her shoulder, and together they ran after the others in a lung-bursting sprint, heading toward the cover of an alley half-choked with a fallen wall.

Behind them, Duseath shouted furious orders. To his right, Kelly saw a contingent of troopers coming with percussion rifles and diehard clones unslung. His mouth went dry. Without weapons they hadn't a prayer of getting out of here. Ahead of him, he saw Phila falter and glance back. Kelly gestured with his free hand.

"Go!" he roared. "Make for the fence."

Even as he said it, he wondered if they could make the gullies beyond the complex. And how long would it take the troopers on patrol scooters to hunt them down?

Beaulieu panted beside him. Her face shone with sweat, and her mouth was open, gulping in air, but her long legs kept stride with his as they dug in and ran harder. Kelly knew they weren't going to make it. They were too exposed, too far behind the others, who had gained the alley.

Overhead, the crosswalks banded shadows across the ground. Glancing up, Kelly saw two troopers standing over him. Neither made any effort to shoot. More games, he thought grimly. Damn them.

Then one of the troopers overhead aimed a long, clumsy weapon that rested upon his shoulder. It looked similar to a flamethrower except no flame belched out of its wide muzzle when he fired. Kelly heard a distinctive *whip, whip, whip* sound. Looking up, he saw the net spreading out as it fell toward them.

"Damn!" he said. "Heads up, Doc."

She looked up and nearly stumbled. "What the—"

The net dropped over them. It was surprisingly heavy, knocking them to the ground. Grunting as he fell, Kelly tried to flatten himself in hopes of squirting out from under the edge of it. But troopers came running up to grasp the weighted ends. They flipped expertly, and Kelly found himself rolled up snugly against the doctor. She was kicking and cursing in fury.

A trooper got too close, and Kelly kicked him hard enough to make him stagger. The net was dragged around, and to his dismay Kelly saw the rest of his squad being brought back, hands on their heads, with armed troopers herding them along.

Coming up and halting near Kelly, Caesar said breathlessly, "Good try, Boss. This just ain't our day."

Kevalyn tried to kneel beside Kelly, but she was shoved away. A trooper seized her by the shoulder and twisted, making her cry out. 41 tried to intervene, and a blow from a rifle butt knocked him to the ground.

"Brutes!" gasped Beaulieu, still struggling. "Inhumane, dirty—"

"Chesez, tut!" bawled a voice.

The troopers parted and Duseath, still holding a cloth to his throat, came through. Kelly glared up at him through the net.

"You flee and twist like a coward," said Duseath, sneering. "Like all humans, you have no concept of the true meaning of death. You are pathetic."

"I know that people have the right to live free on their own worlds without fearing invasion and theft and murder," retorted Kelly. "If I flee from you, it's so I can fight you again and again, until the Salukan Empire learns it cannot conquer the galaxy."

"Silence!" roared Chumiri.

Duseath stepped back. His long face was set and cold. "Minlord, make preparations. I want them impaled."

Chumiri saluted. "Yes, mailord." He turned to the troopers and gestured. "You and you, prepare the poles. You, cut these from the net. They will go first."

A burly trooper with an ill-fitting wig that kept slipping knelt and expertly untwisted the net from around Kelly. He dragged Kelly to his feet, and kicked Beaulieu when she failed to get up quickly enough to suit him. Kelly stepped forward in anger, and the trooper knocked him back with a blow to the mouth. Staggering, Kelly spat out blood and pressed the back of his hand to his mouth.

Chumiri pointed. "Move."

"Not the commander," said Duseath.

Kelly's gaze jerked to his.

Duseath's expression might have been carved from stone. "Let Kelly watch his people die," he said coldly. "Then take him to the ship. He will go back to our pharaon as a prize, and when we are finished taking from him all that he knows he can ride through the streets with me, in a slave collar and chains."

"No!" said Kelly. He jerked free and started toward Duseath, only to be grabbed from behind with his arms held pinned. "Damn you, Duseath. I won't—"

Duseath struck him across the face, reopening the cut.

"What is wrong, Commander? Have you finally realized that it's harder to live than to die?" Duseath raked Kelly with a contemptuous gaze, then turned to Chumiri. "You have your orders, minlord. Kill them now."

14

The sun went down with splashes of coral and gold against an approaching cloud bank of deep indigo. Snow glittered in the yellow light as though ore dust had been sprinkled across its surface. A cold wind billowed cloaks and set Kelly's teeth chattering as they stood near the equipment lot, watching five metal poles being driven into the frozen ground by a smoke-belching pile driver. Kelly managed to tear his gaze away from the sight. He looked at the others.

"I'm sorry," he said. "I let you down."

Phila's dark head snapped up. "Not you, sir," she said fiercely. "Those *cosquenti*, Baker and Siggerson, they let us down."

Beaulieu studied Kelly and leaned close. "How's the headache?" she asked.

He started to shrug off the question, then realized the distraction of going about her duties was probably something she needed right now.

"Just tolerable," he said. "What about 41?"

Together they gazed at the mercenary, who sat on the ground with his head resting on his knees. Blood matted his hair on his right temple. Kelly frowned. He owed this stranger a lot, mostly for Kevalyn's sake but some for his own.

"He's in pain, but very tough," said Beaulieu softly. "Must be his hybrid constitution. Of course if his fever comes back up he won't be. . . ." Beaulieu's voice altered. "Not that it matters . . . now."

The pile driver shut down, and sudden quiet rushed over them. Kelly looked at his squad, feeling the urge to speak, yet knowing that no words could prove adequate. He met Kevalyn's gaze and drew courage from what he found there. Awkwardly, he said to them, "Swift flight, and home again." His voice roughened, and he had to swallow to finish it.

"You too, C-Commander," said Phila.

Kevalyn said something inarticulate and rushed into his arms, hugging him tight so that for a moment his senses filled with the smell and feel of her. He choked, closing his eyes.

"Achei!" shouted the minlord. *"Maitan!"*

Kevalyn jerked from Kelly's arms and stood beside him with her head held high. She had on the Kelly look, that proud, disdainful, go-to-hell expression he and his brothers and sisters had all inherited from their father.

The troopers seized Phila first, dragging her bodily to a pole and lifting her as though she were a child. The wind blew her dark curls across her face so that Kelly could not see her expression. He looked away to the snow-shrouded mountains. He would make the Salukans pay for this, he vowed. Before they broke his mind, he would make them pay.

A tremendous boom in the sky shook the world. It sounded similar to a broken sound barrier, only much louder. Kelly jumped and looked up. The troopers involuntarily lowered Phila, who kicked free and ran.

"Get her!" shouted Duseath.

A trooper lumbered after her. Caesar threw himself in the trooper's path and got swatted to the ground.

"Go, Phila!" yelled Kelly. He swung around, and found a blaster inches from his belly with a watchful trooper on the other end of it.

Someone fired after Phila. She dodged just in time behind a loader, and the shot pinged harmlessly off metal.

"Mailord!" An oparch bolted from the building and came running full tilt, waving his arms. He burst into their midst and halted panting before Duseath. "Mailord, bad news. The defense system has activated. The freighter just exploded. The crew of your cruiser are attempting evacuation—"

A second boom, even louder than the first, shook the world. Eardrums ringing, Kelly took advantage of the confusion to seize the blaster held on him and chop the trooper below the throat. Swinging around Kevalyn, Kelly shot Chumiri, and the minlord toppled with a hoarse scream.

Then there were shots blasting everywhere. Kelly grabbed Kevalyn's arm and dived for the ground, scrambling frantically for cover. He glimpsed 41—blond hair flying in the wind—grappling with a guard. 41 pulled the guard's dagger from his belt and stabbed him with it, then grabbed his blaster and finished the job. Caesar was yelling a war cry that made Kelly's hair stand on end. Salukan curses filled the air, and some of the troopers were deserting despite Duseath's shouts.

Kelly skidded on his knees behind a barrel and drove Kevalyn flat with his hand. "Stay here," he said.

"Wait!" She gripped his sleeve, flinching as a shot rattled the barrel. "Where are you going?"

Kelly saw Duseath darting for cover with a flash of his crimson cloak. "After him. Keep your head down."

Covering himself with a fierce round of the blaster, Kelly zigzagged across the lot. A shot singed past him and marked the poles. Kelly rolled frantically, gained his feet, and kept running. Not only did Duseath have their communicators, but with Chumiri dead he might be the only one in the complex who knew the necessary password to save the miners. Kelly couldn't let him get away.

Glancing back, Duseath fired at Kelly, who dodged behind the blackened remains of a fuel tank. Cautiously Kelly peered around the edge and saw Duseath making for one of the ore carriers. Kelly sighted on him and fired, but Duseath was already beyond the blaster's short range. Swearing, Kelly ran after him.

They were in the open now. Duseath glanced back again, his face a grimace, and quickened speed. Groaning, Kelly dug in deep and sprinted harder, feeling the burn in his muscles as he sought all the speed he had. Duseath's head start made it look like there was no way to catch him. But Kelly forced himself to go faster. He had to get him. He had to.

Duseath reached the carrier and climbed up the ladder to the cab. Flinging open the door, he jumped inside. Seconds later, the engine caught with a spluttering cough and roar. The carrier rolled slowly forward on its gigantic treads. Kelly came pounding up, wheezing as he paralleled the carrier. He jumped the final distance.

Managing to catch a rung of the ladder, he was dragged several feet before he could pull himself up. Duseath, apparently unfamiliar with the operation of the carrier, tried to increase speed too rapidly. The engine screamed in protest and coughed. Something metallic ground in an ear-splitting screech of protest. The carrier staggered, hesitating, then lurched ahead.

Almost dislodged, Kelly hung on grimly. He managed to get up another rung, then his feet found purchase. He reached for the swinging door of the cab and coiled his legs inside.

Duseath tried to shoot him, but Kelly kicked his wrist and the blaster went flying. Kelly kicked again, knocking Duseath sideways.

The carrier slewed around, its treads digging into the frozen ground as it rumbled out of control toward the tents. Duseath caught Kelly's ankle and twisted it savagely. Kelly kicked with his other foot and caught Duseath just above his rib cage. Kelly's heel drove deep into the soft part of Duseath's upper chest, wringing a grunt from the mailord. Duseath collapsed in a heap on the far side of the cab.

Swiftly, Kelly scrambled the rest of the way inside the cab. He reached for the controls, but Duseath clutched his shoulder. Twisting, Kelly slapped away Duseath's hands and seized him by the throat.

At once Kelly realized his mistake, for he'd forgotten the stiff cartilage that protected Duseath's windpipe. Before Kelly could grab for a better hold, Duseath pulled his dagger. Kelly was a fraction slow in blocking the thrust. The dagger point skidded across his ribs, and stinging pain followed in its wake. Kelly punched Duseath in his upper chest where he'd kicked him before. Duseath's eyes rolled up, and his face went a sickly yellow hue.

Kelly shook him hard to keep him from falling unconscious. "Duseath!" he shouted. "What's the password for today's orders? Duseath!"

The mailord's dark blue eyes narrowed in hatred. He grimaced and reached for his mouth. Kelly slapped down his hand.

"Oh no, you don't," he said grimly. "No poison for you. What's the password?"

"Why . . . should I tell you?" gasped Duseath.

"Because I've defeated you."

Duseath managed a faint smile. "From one warrior to another?"

"Yes."

He snorted, then winced in pain. "You presume much for a barbarian."

"What's the password? Come on, Duseath! What's the point in letting them be killed now? You've lost and you know it."

"For the sport of it," whispered Duseath.

Furious, Kelly lifted his hand to strike him, but Duseath caught his wrist. They glared at each other a moment.

"As you say," said Duseath. "I've lost. Interesting. You will keep me prisoner?"

"Yes," said Kelly. "That is our way."

"It is a weak way." Duseath frowned. "I shall give you the word in exchange for your promise."

Kelly swiftly masked his surprise. It was rare for a Salukan to ask for the word of a non-Salukan. "What promise?"

"My dagger . . . sent to my son. So that tradition may continue." Duseath gazed at him without his customary cynicism.

Kelly stared at the priceless dagger still clutched in Duseath's hand. The blade's intricate carving was worn from much polishing and honing over the years, centuries probably.

"You have my word of honor as a Kelly. It will go to your House."

Duseath closed his eyes. "The word is *honauk*."

"Thank you—"

Duseath tried to strike again with the dagger, and Kelly punched him hard. The mailord collapsed unconscious.

Wresting the bloody dagger from his slack hand, Kelly searched him for the communicators. He found two. Fastening one around his wrist, Kelly looked up just in time to seize the steer stick and guide the carrier to the side of the tents away from wounded troopers who were trying to drag themselves out of his way. Avoiding them, Kelly steered the carrier in a clumsy circle, knocking down a porta-shed in the process, and headed back for his people.

He thumbed on the comm. "Kelly to *Wellington*. You guys came just in time."

Static crackled back, then an irate voice came on: "*Wellington* who? She's hours away. This is Siggerson on the *Valiant*. I knew I could reactivate that defense system if I had enough time."

Kelly blinked in surprise, then grinned. "My apologies, Mr. Siggerson," he said. "Well done."

"When do you want to come up?"

Kelly wiped the sweat from his face with the back of his hand. "Just as soon as we find enough wristbands. What is the status on those Salukan vessels?"

"Both destroyed. They were within the defense system, and it is obviously programmed to attack anything in close orbit. I was prudent enough to stay outside."

Kelly recalled Beaulieu's report. "You were inside the first time you tried, weren't you?"

There was a pause. "Uh, yes. I suppose I had some luck that time."

Kelly's brows went up. "That's the understatement of the year. Stand by, Siggerson."

"Will comply."

"Oh, and, Siggerson?"

"Yes?"

"The next time you decide to conduct experiments, do so when the operation of the teleport is not crucial."

There was a long moment of silence, then a subdued Siggerson replied, "Also understood. *Valiant* standing by."

The fighting had stopped when Kelly rumbled back into the lot and lurched to a halt. Opening the cab door, he climbed out cautiously. Without Chumiri and Duseath, the troopers obviously considered saving themselves more important than recovering scattered prisoners.

His squad came warily out of hiding.

"I think they're gone, Boss," said Caesar. He was holding his shoulder. "At least to the other side of the complex. With their ships blown to little pieces and their officers down, the wig-heads won't be too interested in continuing the fight. Rounding them up will be like chasing wild Zanzier cats, though."

Kelly nodded, his gaze sweeping automatically over everyone for a count. Hurrying to a dead trooper, he searched him swiftly but didn't find a comm. He ran to Chumiri, then to a nearby oparch who was moaning in pain. Kelly paused a moment, but the youth was done for. His glassy eyes stared at nothing, and blood was flowing too freely to staunch. Pulling the comm from his pocket, Kelly ran back across the lot.

"41!" he said breathlessly. "The password for all communicator-relayed orders is *hanouk*. Only you can pronounce it correctly. Call those mine overseers and stop the killing. Hurry!"

41's face was pale beneath the blood and dirt streaking it. He took the comm from Kelly and thumbed it on. As soon as a response crackled over, he rattled off a string of commands in gutteral Saluk. Not only did he tell the overseers to release the miners, he gave them curt orders to leave the mines at once and start for the northern mountains in double march.

"Do you dare question the orders of the mailord's own will?" he snapped. "Obey!"

"We leave at once," came the hasty response.

41 broke the connection and handed the comm back to Kelly.

Kelly smiled at him. "Thank you."

Caesar beamed at 41. "Say, Boss. For a merc, he's right handy."

41's tawny eyes flashed fiercely. "You—"

"Don't mind Samms," said Kelly, intervening hastily. "He meant it as a compliment."

"Sure," said Caesar, opening his green eyes to innocent width. "No offense."

41 nodded stiffly and left them. Kelly and Caesar exchanged glances.

"Touchy, ain't he?"

"Very. Your jokes won't work with him." Kelly glanced around and walked back to stand more closely to the ore carrier. "Everyone, keep an eye out for snipers. They may decide they want to fight again."

"Won't the boys on the *Wellington* just love rooting out stinking Salukans," said Caesar with a grin. "I've smelled enough perfume to last me for a year." Beaulieu started probing his shoulder, and he winced. "Just don't let the Wellies take all the credit for rescuing us."

Kelly smiled, unable to hold back his news any longer. "The *Wellington*'s not up there. Siggerson came back."

"Siggerson!" Phila crowded closer, and Caesar shook impatiently away from Beaulieu.

"He didn't get blown to Salukan purgatory?" asked Caesar. He whistled long and low. "I didn't think old Siggie had it in him."

Phila scowled. "He caused us a lot of unnecessary trouble. I am going to tie his guts in a knot when I—"

"You," said Kelly, sympathizing with her but trying not to laugh, "are going to start a search for the rest of our wristbands. I have two. The rest should be in the lab upstairs."

"Right." She nodded and tapped Caesar. "You can help. Come on! What's a little blood trickling down your arm?"

Caesar looked outraged. "Listen to Ironpants here. Ever hear of septic wounds, slag burn infections, splinter torn arteries, tetanus, and gangrene? Just because you came out without a scratch doesn't mean. . . ."

They strode off together, arguing. Beaulieu shook her head. "Youth. After all of this I think I want to get drunk for a week." She pulled gently at the bloody slash in Kelly's tunic.

He glanced down. "It stings like hell, but I think it's just a scratch."

"Um. Looks like it. Bleeding has already stopped."

She lifted her gaze to Kelly's, her dark eyes still full of challenge. "Are all Hawk missions like this?"

"Well, no," he said. "Sometimes they're exciting and a little dangerous."

She snorted.

He said, "Still think you're too old for the job?"

She swung around sharply. "Do you?"

Instead of answering, he said, "You can go back to Harrier division if you want. I didn't make the transfer permanent. After all, I did shanghai you."

Her intake of air was audible. "So. After risking my neck in a snowstorm all night trying to rescue you, I'm still not good enough for the job. Let me tell you, Commander, that I kept up with Operative Mohatsa. No, I did more than keep up. I found us shelter so we didn't die of frostbite, and I did a damned good job of crawling on my belly in knee-high snow under an electrified fence without setting off their security alarms. I also picked locks and executed some preventative medicine with my diehard before we got captured. If you think you can bounce me back and forth with arbitrary transfers so that after all of this I end up puttering around the central quadrant with some commander assigned to diplomatic escorts and courier service, forget it. You got me, and I'm staying. I can run rings around any of—''

Kelly threw up his hands. ''Whoa, Doctor! You've convinced me you want to stay.''

''Why wouldn't I want to—'' She broke off, her expression changing abruptly. ''I see,'' she said much more quietly. ''I did throw a fit when I first came aboard, didn't I?''

Kelly smiled. ''A pretty impressive fit.''

She smiled back wryly. ''The medical profession tends to spawn prima donnas. Make my assignment a permanent one, please.''

Kelly put out his hand and they shook. Her clasp was firm.

He said, ''You might take a look at the mailord in the cab. I hit him pretty hard. Check him for any poison caches. They usually like to keep it in a tooth. We're going to take him in as a prisoner. West seldom gets an officer of his rank to question.''

Beaulieu's gaze sharpened. ''You sound as though you'd like to be in on that questioning session. What happened with the mind sieve?''

Kelly sobered. ''We'll discuss it later.''

''Not many survive it, you know. You should be glad.''

''Yeah.'' He stared in the distance, remembering it with a resurgence of anger and resentment. Beaulieu waited a moment, then started to climb up to the carrier cab. He broke from his reverie. ''Doc.''

She glanced back over her shoulder.

He frowned. ''Your other observations. That . . . private report to West. Am I still Killer Kelly?''

Her impatient eyes softened. ''Not in my report. And as far as I can tell, you never were. How would you rate your own performance?''

He glanced up at that, but with a slight smile she turned and climbed into the cab without waiting for his answer. Kelly stared after her. He had come through the cloud that had been haunting him since the funerals. Maybe that was enough for now.

Turning, he saw Kevalyn standing a slight distance apart with 41. She was saying something Kelly could not hear. 41 stood half-turned away from her, looking both wary and fascinated. Kevalyn smiled, turning on the famous Kelly charm, and held out her hand. 41 hesitated, frowning, and Kevalyn dropped hers.

"I'm sorry," she said clearly enough for Kelly to hear her. "I forgot you don't shake hands."

41 stared at her in silence, his dirty face a mixture of flitting expressions Kelly could not read. Then he touched her chin with the tips of his fingers, tilting up her head a bit. Kelly stepped forward involuntarily, but 41 had already swung away. He walked from Kevalyn, who watched him with wry puzzlement on her face.

Kelly went to her, and she took his arm with a sigh. "Well, my appeal must be slipping."

Kelly gripped the dagger a little more tightly. "I'd have socked him."

"For kissing me?" She burst out laughing. "Are all brothers raised in the Dark Ages? I would expect that sort of comment from Drew but not you, kid. I'm an old divorced lady, remember?"

"He's a mercenary, half Salukan and God knows what else, and doesn't even have a name," said Kelly, but he was grinning ruefully at himself. "Yeah, you're right. How're you doing, Kevie? Did this backwater help you straighten yourself out?"

Her gray eyes suddenly filled with tears. "I was getting there. Rege—the man Chumiri killed—was special." She choked and gripped Kelly's sleeve.

Gently he put his arm around her and held her tight for a moment. "I'm sorry," he whispered.

She shook herself. "Yeah. More hard work, I suppose." She wiped the tears from her face. "Damn them! Why can't they understand peace? Are they really such monsters?"

"No," said Kelly, gazing down at the dagger in his hand. "Not monsters. Just fathers, husbands, and sons who don't recognize us as anything higher than animals. I don't know why. We may never be able to break that wall."

She sniffed. ''I owe my life to 41.''

''I know. Several times over. We both owe him.'' Kelly hugged her again. ''I wouldn't have really socked him.''

She almost managed a smile. ''He didn't want my thanks. He acts sometimes as though he's never been around other people at all, and yet he seems to like us. Have you noticed?''

''Yes.'' Kelly smiled into her eyes. ''Ready to go home?''

She blinked and pulled away in surprise. ''No! Are you crazy? Your shelling flattened my lab. I'll have to start all over with my samples. Six months' work down the—''

''Now wait,'' he broke in with a frown. ''You can't stay here with—''

''Why not? When those cruisers get here, there's going to be a lot of work ahead of us. We've got to get those people out of the mines. They'll need medical treatment and convalescent care. Housing will have to be erected in addition to recreating all the labs. The data they destroyed, Bryan! It makes me burn. And my entire staff is still down in the bottom of Long Sally. I can't just go off and leave everything in a mess.''

He sighed and gave up. Kevalyn kissed his cheek and began asking Beaulieu questions about a procedure Kelly couldn't make any sense of. He looked at 41, leaning against the treads of the parked carrier. The mercenary looked tired and very alone. Kelly hesitated, then walked over to him.

''We made a deal,'' he said. ''I intend to keep it. We can drop you off at Station 4 or anywhere else on the way.''

For a moment 41 made no response at all, then his amber eyes shifted to look at Kevalyn. ''She will not go with you.''

Kelly sighed. ''No, stubborn to the core, that's my sister. I guess it's a Kelly trait.''

41 blinked. ''Sister?''

''Yes. Older by four years.''

41 smiled briefly to himself, looking a little brighter. He said nothing more, however.

After a moment Kelly shifted his feet and said, ''Well? Where do you want a lift to?''

''Do Hawks hire mercenaries?''

Surprised, Kelly looked at him eagerly. 41 would be invaluable to Spec. Ops., but Kelly never dreamed he would even consider joining.

"No, they don't," he said. "But they do let mercenaries join."

41 frowned. "How long is a hitch?"

"Four years. There's training for six weeks—"

"I don't need training."

Kelly raised his brows, but went on smoothly: "Plenty of leave time. Good pay. Lots of hard work."

"Like this?"

Kelly grinned. "Yeah. Like this." He hesitated a moment, then said, "I happen to be short-handed with Baker dead. I think I could pull a string or two with the commodore and get you assigned to my squad. If you don't like it, you can always transfer to another commander."

41 grunted. "Orders. Discipline." He shook his head. "I dislike such things. I dislike idealists like you . . . like your sister. No, Kelly. No joining."

Kelly hid his disappointment. With a shrug he started to turn away. "As you wish."

"Wait." 41 took a step toward him. "The Hawks, they would distrust me."

Kelly waited.

"My Salukan blood is obvious." 41's face twisted. "A thing of shame. To live with humans is . . . difficult. Their ways are odd to me. I don't always know the right thing to do."

Such an admission wasn't easy to make. Kelly looked at him with a new measure of respect. "I can't say you won't meet prejudice," he said at last. "I didn't trust you at first. You'll hit that a lot. You'll have to learn to deal with it. But if you check out, you'll be trusted by the operatives you have to work with and depend on."

41 stared at him like a wild thing that wants a home but is afraid to trust enough to come inside. "Check out? The Alliance version of a mind sieve?"

Kelly grimaced at the memory. "Not exactly. It doesn't hurt."

"I heard the troopers talking," said 41. "You gave the mailord the Alliance transmissions code when you were being tortured."

A smile touched Kelly's lips. He met 41's eyes. "I gave him *a* code. I think, if the Salukans try to use it, that they will be on the entertainment frequency used by Boxcan shipping merchants for their crews. Many long lectures on how to polish deck plates and how many children the ideal family unit should produce."

41 did not smile, but the wariness seemed to fade from his eyes. He cocked his head. "You are a clever man, Kelly."

"Commander!"

Kelly turned and saw Phila and Caesar returning. Phila gave him a thumbs up signal. He saw the wristbands in her hand, and both of them were carrying recovered diehards. Kelly nodded in approval and activated his comm.

"Kelly to *Valiant*. Come in, please."

"*Valiant* here," said Siggerson promptly.

"We're preparing to come up. Can you take my coordinates from this position?'

There was a pause. "Coordinates registered and locked in. Standing by for your signal."

"Good," said Kelly. He glanced at his sister and gave her his spare wristband. "Kevalyn, at least come aboard with us until the cruisers arrive."

She smiled. "Yes, I'll be glad to. I want to see your new ship. Caesar's been telling me what happened to the last one. You'd better be more careful in the future."

41 frowned. "What did happen to it?"

"Shot to pieces," said Caesar, handing a wristband to Beaulieu. "Like we thought happened to this one."

"Ah, I remember," said 41. "Baker spoke of it."

"Baker?" said Caesar indignantly. "What did that brig bilge know? He wasn't on the Dexos mission. He—"

"Never mind," said Kelly. He did a quick count of wristbands and people and frowned. "We started out with five. I see only four, including mine."

"Mine got blown up," said Caesar.

Kelly unfastened his wristband so the teleport connection was broken. "Siggerson, take up two. And we'll need three more wristbands sent down. We're short."

"Acknowledged. Uh, Kelly?"

"Yes?"

"About that ghost reading on my sensors—"

Kelly sighed. "Haven't you tracked that glitch down yet?"

"As a matter of fact, I have." Siggerson's voice hesitated. "It's a ouoji. A Minzanese ship's mascot, considered by tradition to bring good luck."

Kelly blinked in surprise. The others gathered around.

"What's a wo-gee?" asked Caesar. "What's it look like?"

"I wanted to be sure we can keep it," said Siggerson. "It's probably against regulations, but it's quite clean and intelligent. And this is a Minzanese ship in spite of the name change."

"A pet?" asked Phila with dawning glee. "Siggerson wants to keep a pet? Does this mean he is human?"

Kelly made a hushing motion with his hand. "We seem to have needed that good luck, Mr. Siggerson. I have no objections to the ouoji, providing—"

"Yes, sir," broke in Siggerson quickly. "Ready to teleport two now."

Beaulieu and Kevalyn dematerialized. Seconds later, three wristbands twinkled into existence upon the ground. Kelly picked them up while Caesar and Phila dragged the unconscious Duseath from the cab. Phila took a wristband for herself then fastened one on the mailord. Kelly handed one to Caesar, then glanced at 41 and hesitated.

"Well?" said Kelly. "Are you coming with us, or not?"

A sniper shot rang out, pinging off the carrier over 41's head and making them all duck. Kelly tossed the wristband at 41, and he fastened it on.

"Yes," he said. "I will come."

"Good." Kelly smiled. "Siggerson, we're ready to come home. Bring us all up."